Twisted Up In Us– Treyton Sisters Novel

By

Dawn Martens

Twisted Up In Us

Broken hearted and in need of an escape, Melissa turns to her newfound father, Hangman, president of the Untamed MC. Everything about her relationship with Dray was founded on lies. Lies she is desperate to forget.

Dray is determined to set the story straight and win back her love and trust no matter the cost. Only there is a kink in his plan in the name of Slammer.

A member of the Untamed who has never been faithful, until he lays his eyes on Melissa.

Dray and Slammer both want her, but only one man can have her heart…

Who will win in this tangled game of love and war?

This story is told in 3 different POV's and a few POV's from Hangman!

This book is NOT a standalone, you MUST read Twisted Up In You and Always Was Mine FIRST.

DAWN MARTENS

Copyright © Dawn Martens

Published 2018

Cover Art by Glenna Maynard

Edited by Emily Snow

Proof Read by Michelle Simm and Michelle Barlow Price

Formatted by Glenna Maynard

Twisted Up In Us is a work of fiction. All names, characters, places and events portrayed in this book either are from the author's imagination or are used fictitiously. Any similarity to real persons, living or dead, establishments, events, or location is purely coincidental and not intended by the author. Please do not take offence to the content, as it is FICTION.

Trademarks: This book identifies product names and services known to be trademarks, registered trademarks, or service marks of their respective holders, the author acknowledges the trademarked status in this work of fiction. The publication and use of these

Dedication

To all my readers, especially those that have been waiting so long for Melissa's story

Acknowledgments

This is usually the hardest part, but it's actually quite easy for me.

As always, my G-baby, Glenna Maynard, you're my best friend, and I appreciate you more than words could ever say. Thank you for everything you do for me, even when you give me 'homework'. Loves and kisses!

To Emily Snow, my poop-face, thank you for just simply being my friend, even when I'm crazy and threaten to show you my tits.

And to Michelle and Angie– thank you for always looking over my stuff and telling me what to fix and how to fix it.

Note from the Author

As some may know, I started writing this book in 2015, right as I finished writing Cori's book, Twisted Up In You. However, this book has haunted me, taking forever to fully come to life, what with all my health issues and of course writer's block. But it's finally done. This book is not only the conclusion to The Treyton Sisters Duet, but it's also a sneak peak into the Untamed MC. I hope you enjoy!

Prologue

Dray

Standing at the front of the church, waiting for Melissa to walk down the aisle to me, I'm nervous. I tried to get her to marry me before our daughter came, but she was stubborn. Said no way. Mostly because she didn't want to be a pregnant bride, and because she wanted us to work on our relationship before we took it to this level.

Thankfully, after a tongue-lashing where her sister, Cori, told her to stop being stubborn, Melissa finally agreed to marry me. Of course, when I went to Angel, Zippo, and Reaper for permission, they put me through the ringer. Reaper kept cleaning his knives and his gun in front of me as I nervously asked for their blessing.

There are still things Melissa doesn't know about me, but my boss told me I couldn't tell her just yet, because it would ruin a four-year investigation. And I can't fuck that up. I also hate lying to my woman. I know she'd keep it to herself, if she knew the truth, but if my boss ever found out she knew before we closed the case, I would lose my job.

The music starts up and I see her, my angel, my beautiful Melissa walking toward me, carrying our daughter Mikayla on her hip. *Fuck,* she's beautiful.

Angel puts Melissa's hand in mine after taking Mikayla from her and goes to sit down so we can start.

Then it happens, everything is destroyed—my whole world comes crashing down. What should be the start of my life with Melissa ends before it ever truly begins.

Hangman from the Untamed Angels MC, storms into the church, followed by his men. Angel instantly hands Mikayla back to Melissa as the clubs face off.

"You didn't think to tell me I had a daughter?" Hangman roars, glaring at Jasper. He looks to Melissa quickly, eyes settling on my daughter. "A granddaughter?"

"How'd you find out?" Angel answers back.

"How do you think? I finally get my wife back, and not only am I just finding out that I have a daughter who is twenty years old, but my brother—who not only is alive—also got *my wife* pregnant and is living with your pussy club!"

Shit. This isn't good.

I see Trevor tense up. This is a moment that he's avoided for years. Being in the company of his brother. Hangman is so terrible; the guy faked his death to get away from him.

"This isn't the time or place for this," Jasper declares, throwing his hands out.

"No, it's the perfect fucking time." *Motherfucker*. I would recognize that voice anywhere. My ex-wife moves from her spot behind Hangman. "You son of a bitch, what do you think you are doing, huh?"

"Shayla…" I start to say but Melissa cuts me off.

"Um, I'm sorry, but who are you?"

"Who am I? Well, this is great. Now, I actually feel bad for you," Shayla says, sounding at least half human for once. "*I'm his wife*," she cries out, managing to appear distraught.

God, I hate this woman.

"Wife?" Melissa chokes out as if she were just punched in the stomach. She looks to me to deny Shayla's claims, but I can't. Not entirely. We were married but that was the past.

"I never signed his stupid ass papers, so he probably didn't realize we're still married. I told him before what my conditions were. He visits his children, talks to them. Then, and only then, would I let him be free," she says, tears forming in her eyes. And there we have it, the bitch fake cries. As usual.

3

Her hand goes to her throat and she continues with the act. She looks at the beautiful life Melly and I made. "You had his child?"

With that, Melissa takes off crying as soon as Cori runs to her taking Mikayla. I watch Cori and Blake follow her quickly out of the church doors.

"Melissa! Stop please," I yell out for her. Everyone is holding me back from going to her and I see Shayla's face. The cunt has the nerve to smirk. Not sure what the fuck she's playing at here, but I will end her.

"You hurt my kid, you motherfucker. Why shouldn't I hurt you?" Hangman roars at me.

Everything is in chaos, Hangman gets a punch in, and the Angels all stare at me with disgust.

"Hangman, we get shit is bad right now. Everyone calm down and we'll ride to the clubhouse and have a talk. Clear the air," Angel says, being the peacemaker.

"I'll be keeping my eye on you," Hangman warns me one final time and storms out.

Shayla still stands there, smirking her smug bitchy smirk. She has once again destroyed my whole world. She has another thing coming though if she thinks I'm letting her off so easy this time.

Chapter 1

Melissa

Can this week get any worse? First my wedding day was ruined when I found out that Dray had a whole other family. How could I not have known that he had another family, another life? How could he have not mentioned that he had other children?

As if that wasn't enough, my father, the man I never knew, the one that didn't even know I existed, showed up, bringing along the estranged wife of the two-timing, dick-faced asshole.

How Dray thought we could get married was beyond me. Didn't he know our marriage wouldn't be legal? Didn't he know he'd most likely go to prison for bigamy?

Dray has tried calling me, multiple times a day. Leaving me countless text messages and voicemails. But I delete each and every one of them without reading or listening to them. I don't want to hear his excuses. There is nothing he can say to defend what he has done. He lied to me.

That's not love.

I finish packing up the last of our things and drag the bags to the front door. "What are you doing, Melly?" Cori asks, looking worried. I love my sister, more than anything. She's happily married now, with a child of her own on the way, and I don't want her to worry about me anymore. She's worried over me since we were children.

"Um, Carson said I could live with him," I say hesitantly. Discovering who my father was, was a shock, but at least now both Cori and I finally know, considering our bitch mom was never going to tell us.

Her brows furrow in concern. "You don't even know this guy. And from what the guys say, he's bad news."

I shrug. "I know, okay, I know. But even Tori vouched for him, saying he was a good father, so at least that's something. And this will be like a getting to know you sort of thing. I just need to get away. Somewhere Dray won't look for me. I can't stay here and be reminded of him day in and day out."

Tears well up in her eyes. "Remember though, that's Dray's daughter too. He might be an asshole right now, but you can't shut him out of her life." Being pregnant and married sure has changed Cori. Gone is her snarky personality—it's like she was replaced by an alien.

6

"He doesn't give a shit about his other kids, doubt he'll care about her. I'm not putting her through that. He can kiss my ass," I tell her angrily. She should know how this feels; we both grew up with missing fathers that never gave a fuck to even find out about us. I'm not putting Mikayla through that pain.

I can tell Cori wants to say more but instead just gives me a sad smile. She comes to me, pulling me tight for a hug. "Call me? Often?"

"Of course," I choke out, my face resting on her shoulder. "I'll come back…eventually. I promise. I just need to go. I can't be here right now." I can't chance running into Dray. He made a fool of me.

Cori helps me down to the front of the building with my bags, while I carry Mikayla and her suitcase. Carson, my dad, is standing against his truck waiting for us. He calls it a cage, which is strange to me, but whatever. He takes everything from Cori and me, telling me to get in. He still kind of scares me. I never would have known that he and Trevor were brothers, because they look nothing alike. They have the same height but where Trevor is a scrawny hipster, Carson is built more like a bodybuilder. Long shaggy brown hair and a giant messy beard. I almost wonder if I could convince him to get a haircut and a beard trim. Because he looks like something out of a horror movie right now.

Buckling Mikayla up, I turn back to Cori, giving her one last hug goodbye. "Don't tell Dray, please. Just let him know I'm gone if he keeps harassing."

Cori nods and kisses me on the cheek.

"I'll miss you, both of you," Cori tells me as she steps away from the truck, waving and blowing kisses to Mikayla.

Carson gives my sister a grin paired with a wink, and we leave. Off to the other side of the country to get away from Dray and to finally have a father.

Chapter 2

Melissa

Took a week, but we're finally here. We had to stop more often because of Mikayla, but Carson didn't seem to mind. My father's house looks typical, not what I was expecting at all. We didn't really talk much on the drive; it was sort of awkward. But thankfully Mikayla babbled away in the back seat and entertained us for most of the drive.

Carson walks me into his house and I look around. It's simple, and there isn't anything illegal here, at least not what I can see. It looks basic, even basic colors of brown and grey on the walls all around. From standing in the entry way I can see there is a basement that looks like it's unfinished.

Walking down the hall, I notice a large family room connected to a dining room, then kitchen. Going to the left is another hallway with a large bathroom and a few bedrooms.

"Mikayla's room is right here. Had the guys come while we drove to get it done up. I told those fucks she was just a baby so not to get anything she could choke on." He opens the door and its painted pink with white stripes. There's a toddler bed all set up in the middle of the room, it even has a *Frozen* canopy. The bed has so many stuffed toys on it that it makes me wonder if there'll be room for Mikayla to sleep in it. At the end of the bed is a toy box overflowing with so many toys that I swear they must have went to Toys R Us and bought the store out.

And of course, for a final touch, there's a pink TV anchored on the wall.

"Wow." Mikayla squirms in my arms, wanting down. She waddles over to the toys on the floor and plops down to play. I smile up at my father. "You didn't have to do all this."

"Yeah, sort of did, kid. You're mine, I take care of what's mine," he says gruffly. He pulls me along to another room, just beside Mikayla's and opens that door. "This is yours. I wasn't sure what you were into, but Cori told me you were a fan of reds and black, so I passed that shit onto the guys and they did this."

Looking around, I want to cry. It's so beautiful. The walls to the left and right are black, the walls that my bed is against and at my back are red. There is a plush red and black bedding set on the bed and a huge TV is mounted on the wall. A black dresser with the handles painted red, and a giant red-trimmed mirror is against the black wall to the left.

"This looks amazing. Oh my god." I breathe.

"Glad you like it, kid," he says, ruffling my hair. This interaction feels awkward to me, but it doesn't seem to phase him. It's like he's always done this. "When's the baby got to nap?"

I check the time, it's a little after twelve. "I need to get her lunch and then she can go down for one."

"Good, we'll talk when she's asleep." He stomps away and starts banging away in the kitchen. I take another look at my room and smile. I can't believe he went to all this trouble, just for me. I pull my cell phone out and take pictures of both rooms and send them to Cori.

Holy shit! Maybe he's not so bad after all - C

I smile as I type, *Yeah. Maybe. Maybe he's not.*

Grabbing Mikayla out of her room, I carry her into the kitchen and find that there is a highchair at the table. "You really didn't have to go all out like this," I say as I strap her in.

Carson shrugs, mumbling something under his breath and hands me a plate for myself. "Mind if I feed her?" he asks.

Staring at him in shock, all I can do is nod my head, even though she pretty much feeds herself now. And by feeding herself, I mean she just uses her hands to eat. What big scary biker man wants to feed a baby? Studying my face, he chuckles, like he knew exactly what I was thinking. I quickly sit down as I feel my face get warm.

"It's not much, the guys got a bunch of take out shit last night and put it all in the fridge," he says as I dig into the fried rice and chicken balls on my plate.

Chapter 3

Melissa

Lunch was interesting, watching Carson feeding Mikayla was the highlight for sure. I think he got more food in his beard and hair than in her mouth. He shot me a glare when I giggled. After she was somewhat fed, he got her out of the chair, cleaned her up, and put her down for her nap. I was surprised.

The stories I've heard from Tori and the guys made me terrified of him, but *damn,* he's good with kids.

He comes back as I put my plate in the dishwasher and asks me to join him in the living room. Sitting on the couch, I start getting nervous.

"I want to know everything, Melissa. About your time in the foster system, to how the Angels came to find you, to what it all has to do with your mother. *Especially* about your mother."

I start the story, filling him in on the abuse mom gave Cori and I. How she abandoned us, and we went to foster care, how she pulled us back out of the system a few times only to send us back. The last home we were in and how Cori and her friend, Chelsea, found the Angels to save us. I tell him about watching Cori getting raped, then pregnant, then how I watched them take the baby away from her. I tell him about growing up in the Angels' safehouse, how they are my family. How we recently found out the baby Cori gave birth to had died.

Everything.

When I'm done, he sits there in silence, anger etched into his face. "You said your mother was arrested on her last visit to you guys."

I nod.

"You know who I am, right? What I do?"

I gulp and nod again.

"If she dies or simply…goes missing, will you care?"

My eyes bug out. "I uh, I don't know. Whatever you do, please don't tell me." I don't need to know if he is going to commit a crime because that would make me an accessory.

He gives me a chin lift and stands up. "I need to go to the club house. Rule I have: family never goes there. I don't want to catch you there. If do, there'll be problems."

I look at him in shock. "Really? No family ever? No family cookouts, nothing?" I'm not used to that; the Angels' club house was always open and welcoming to everyone.

"We're bikers, we fuck, fight, party and have our dealings. We have family things, sure, but at our houses, never the club house." He pauses at the front door before turning around. "You want a massage or other spa shit done, you tell me first, I'll set something up. I never want to catch you at a spa in this town, got me?" Again, my eyes bug out and I nod. I heard about his spas, they specialize in happy endings. *Yuck.*

"Now that your paternity has been solved, any idea who your sister's dad is?"

I nod. "Mom never told us. Whenever we used to ask, she would tell us to shut up, but Cori finally learned that her dad is Sam Mayer."

His brows shoot up in surprise. "So, she's related by blood then to the Angels," he states and then mumbles, "Everyone is fuckin' related to them these days," as he walks out. I bite my lip to keep from laughing. He's officially related to one as well, considering his brother, Trevor is a member.

He leaves and I'm still processing some of the things he told me and I'm back to scared again. I shoot a text to Cori letting her know what just happened and she calls me right away.

"Holy shit! Are you sure you want to stay there? We can come get you, bring you back home."

I smile. "No, I want to stay, just for a while. I'll come home, don't worry, but I just found my dad. I know he's scary as fuck, but I want to get to know him. Plus, I want to change him," I say as I laugh.

"Girl, he's almost forty, he's set in his life, he isn't going to change. If he couldn't change for Tori, whom he claimed to love, he ain't gonna change for you."

This is true. "Oh, I know, but I can be a cockblocker, I'm good at that."

That has Cori laughing.

"That you are good at. Okay, well, call me once a week, text me everyday. If you don't, I'm coming down there to hurt you."

We say goodbye, and I pull my phone away and smile. Mikayla will be asleep for another hour, so I decide to just lay on the couch and watch some TV. My cell phone chimes with a text and I see it's from Trevor.

You get there safe?

Yes, Uncle Trevor. – M

That's still weird to hear. But I'm glad.

How's Tori? – M

Watching some shitty day time soap opera

16

I laugh.

I'm glad you have her back -M

Me too

I put my phone on the coffee table and lay on the couch just thinking while the TV plays in the background. I rub at my eyes, grab my laptop, and try to do some research on Dray and his wife. I hate this. I know there is more to the story. Maybe Dray really did think he was divorced, but either way, why didn't he just tell me. I wouldn't have cared.

If he was just honest, I would still be with him right now, maybe trying for another child. He'd help me with midnight feedings.

We'd be happy still.

Chapter 4

Hangman

I get to the club house and round the brothers up for Church.

"First order of business. Club name. I'm sick as fuck of being compared to them damned Angels Warriors," I tell my brothers as I lean back in my chair.

"Same, someone hears Untamed Angels and they think of those fuckin' pussies," Rage mutters from his seat off to the side of me.

"All in favor of dropping the Angels from our name? We'll be the Untamed MC."

Aye's go around the table, not one person voted against it.

"Second, my daughter: not one of you fuckers touches her, not unless you can be the man she deserves. I know our lifestyle, cheating is our nature, but my little girl needs a man that can keep his dick in check and be what she needs, not only for herself, but for her daughter. She's been hurt more than enough in her life, and I won't allow it to continue. Hurt my girl, I'll kill you."

"Got it, Pres," everyone shouts at the same time.

"Well fuck, there goes my plans of trying out some new pussy," Gamer jokes from the end of the table.

The room goes quiet and everyone looks at me, waiting for my reaction. "The fuck you just say?" I ask slowly as I pull out my gun from its holster.

Gamer shoves back, holding his hands up, "Pres, I was just joking, brother. I'll stay away from your daughter."

"Good, lets party."

I bang my gavel to end the meeting and go in search of some pussy. Fuck knows I need it after being on the road for a week with my kid and granddaughter. But before I leave the room, I punch Gamer in the face and he goes down, nose bleeding, "Don't joke about my kid like that. Next time, it won't be a fuckin' punch, I'll shoot you."

Chapter 5

Dray

3 weeks later

Three weeks, my life went to shit three weeks ago, and I can't seem to fix it. I thought for sure Shayla and I were over. I signed those papers, she signed them, but as I've come to find out, she didn't file the damn papers. I don't know why, not a clue. Turns out the bitch even sent me a fake letter saying the divorce was finalized. Just so I wouldn't know the truth. I pulled out the divorce decree and looked it over, it looks legit, it's why I never questioned it. But sure enough, when I called the courthouse to investigate it, they said I was indeed married. The bitch must have gotten help from my fucking brother with the fake papers.

I gave her everything she asked for in the divorce. Full custody, the house, everything. I should have known something was going on when she started calling a few months ago, but I ignored it because she's all about drama, and I'm done falling into her shit.

Last night I agreed to meet up with her, to see the kids. Her and my brother deserve each other but can't be together cos that dick is already married with kids and won't divorce Layla. Layla doesn't know about his affairs; the money he has in a secret account that he gives to the other women. She doesn't even know about his children with *my* damn wife.

I told Shayla last night I would be telling the kids everything. They're ten and thirteen now, they can finally understand the truth. Shayla said if I told them they would hate her, but that's not my problem. She's had years to tell them the truth. I know I should have told them a long ass time ago, but I couldn't bear to do it. Seeing them hurt killed me. I've always wanted a bunch of kids, and knowing that the ones I raised weren't mine, *fuck*. I'm tearing my brother's life apart for ruining mine, and I'll take great joy in it.

I worked years to get my intel on him, being undercover, and I finally have the file. I have shit on just about everyone. Randy even knows my real work, it's why he put me as bouncer in his club instead of one of his men, since it looks less suspicious.

Only reason I stayed in the position, even after men were caught, was because no one knows I'm a cop. It's better this way. Lets me continue doing undercover work without blowing my cover.

Melissa doesn't know, and I hate that I haven't told her. I wanted to so badly, but I also know she'd have told her sister. Cori would have then told Blake, then the Angels would know. My cover would be blown. I should have told her about my wife and those kids though. I tried explaining in a voicemail about how they weren't mine, but I know her, she's stubborn, worse than her sister, so she probably just deleted the messages without listening to them.

I'll get Melissa back, I know I will, but it will take time. In the meantime, I'll get rid of Shayla for good and hopefully help Layla leave my asshole brother.

Flashback Chapter

Dray

The Truth Comes Out

The wait for the god damned test results are taking too long. Both Shayla, Luca, and I all tested to see who's a match. Shouldn't the tests be done? My little girl is in that room right now fighting some fucked up infection that has destroyed one of her kidneys.

Shayla cries into my shoulder quietly, something she's been doing a lot of since I found her sleeping with my brother Matt. I always thought cheating would be something I would never forgive someone for, but after hard work, I managed to move on from it and forgive her, mostly for the sake of our kids.

I also never told Layla, Matt's wife, about the affair either. She didn't need that hurt on her and her children either. Although it still kills every time I see my brother, feel like killing him every time. Shayla of course thinks I'm still holding a grudge about it, and maybe I am, because I haven't touched her sexually since.

And now here we are, in this damn waiting room months later, all of us, the entire family waiting to find out what will happen to our daughter.

I look up as I see the doctor coming down the hall. His face doesn't look like he has any good news. I stand up, pulling Shayla up with me, leaving Luca sitting on the chair.

"Well?"

"I'm afraid none of you are a match," those words feel like a kick to my gut, how could none of us be a match for her? "However, we did test another, and he's a perfect match and he's agreed to donate his kidney for her."

I frown, "Who else did you test?" Shayla fidgets against my side.

"Your brother, Matt, is currently in the operating room as we speak. It shouldn't take too long, but once he's finished, we're start right away with Laura."

I'm stunned, after all the hateful shit going on between Matt and I lately, I never thought he would be the one we ended up needing to save my daughter's life.

An hour later Laura gets wheeled out for surgery, and I give her a kiss on the cheek, letting her know everything will be alright.

"I'm gonna go get something to eat, all this waiting is killing me." I tell Shayla.

"Okay, Luca and I will go in and check on Matt, make sure he's okay and to thank him. Can you bring us back a little something? Maybe a sandwich and an apple?"

"Yeah, no problem." I stare at her, she's not making eye contact with me. Something's up.

As I walk away and head down to the food court, something sinks in. How was Matt a match? It doesn't make sense. I'm Laura's father, Luca is her brother, Shayla her mother, it should have been one of us, right? Unless Shayla's affair was going on much fucking longer than I thought.

No, Laura is my daughter. She has to be.

I spot the doctor that told us about the test results in the food court, eating his lunch, and I walk over to him. "Mr. Hante, what can I do for you?" he asks, as I take a seat next to him.

"Those results of the test, got me thinking, is there any way to do a DNA test? Recently found out my wife had an affair, and for those tests results to not come back as me being a match has my head going into overdrive. I need to know."

He looks at me with sympathy, giving me a sad smile. "I can certainly get the tests ordered up, but just so you are aware, just because you weren't a match doesn't mean you aren't her father. I see cases like this all the time. Twin siblings not being a match, biological parents not being a match, sometimes ends up being a perfect match with a complete stranger."

I nod, "I understand that, I just need to know. While we're doing Laura's test, can we check my son too? I never thought this was something I would be compelled to do, but my gut is telling me I have to." I forgave Shayla for cheating, but I won't be able to forgive her if she's not only been doing it the entire time we've been together, but most especially if my kids aren't mine. That will kill me.

"Absolutely, give me an hour, and you bring the boy down to my office, we'll get it all done up."

I shake his head as I stand up, "Thank you, doctor."

I walk off, quickly grabbing Shayla and Luca some food, and head back up to the waiting area.

Two weeks later, my answers came in the mail.

Chapter 6

Dray

"Captain Spurl," my Boss answers.

"Dray," I reply.

"What can I do for you? You have anything?"

"Sure do. Everything."

He goes quiet. "This is your brother, you still sure you want to go through with this?"

"Yeah, more so now than before. I'm bringing him down and finally telling the truth. You're gonna have to take me out of undercover shit because it'll be blown."

"Shit. You sure? Because you're the best man I have, plus you're the only undercover officer that keeps his dick away from the women you investigate. Makes for less paperwork." He's got that right, for the first few years, I was married, so I wasn't going there. Although that didn't stop a few of the other married UC's. I take my job seriously, always have. Fucking was off limits. Even after I thought I was divorced, I

27

would never dirty my cock inside a woman connected to my cases.

"I'm sure, sir, find me another position in the department." I click off before he can respond and pull in behind Shayla's car.

The house looks the same. It should, considering my brother pays for the upkeep. I knock on the front door and it opens instantly. Laura, my thirteen-year-old niece stares at me in shock. "Dad?" she whispers out. Hearing her call me dad has my chest feeling tight. She rushes to me for a hug. Damn this kills me, knowing I'm about to squash her dream of having me home. I'm the only 'dad' her and Luca have ever known, so this shit has me hating Shayla even more.

"Hey, kid. Luca here too?" I ask, referring to her little brother.

She nods her head. "Mom has been fretting all day, now I know why."

I give her a chin lift. "We need a family meeting."

"Are you coming back home?"

I rub the back of my neck and shake my head. "Your mom and I need to talk with you guys about something important. Something you all should have known a long time ago."

Tears form in her eyes. "This doesn't sound good," she says timidly, too smart for her own good.

I follow behind her into the sitting room and see Luca playing video games. Shayla comes out of the kitchen and Laura was right, she looks scared as shit.

"Luca," I call to him.

His head snaps up so fast I swear he got whiplash. He narrows his eyes at me and glares. "You."

"Turn it off, we all need a family chat."

"We don't want you back here," he snarls at me.

"Trust me, I'm not back. Just here for a chat." He flinches as if I slapped him. *Fuck*, I need to work on my people skills.

We all sit around the table, and I look to Shayla. "You want to say anything before I do, because I'm not pussy-footing around this shit."

She shakes her head, and tears leak out from her eyes.

"What's going on? Please tell us," Laura pleads.

"You know why I left all them years ago?" I start.

Laura gives a slight shake. "I just knew there was lots of fighting."

Luca snorts. "He left cos he's a dick. 'Nuff said."

"Watch the attitude and the language!" I snap. "I left because your mother cheated."

"What?" the kids ask in outrage.

"Mom said you cheated," Laura says quietly as she stares at her mother.

"Never cheated. I loved your mother. Found her with my brother."

Luca glares at his mother as Laura finally looks away, looking down to her lap.

"I was forgiving, stayed, trying to work it out with her, until I found out something I couldn't forgive, ever. I filed for divorce, I thought it was all done, over with. I met someone, love of my life that woman, but because the divorce decree your mother mailed to me was a fake, I couldn't marry her. Our wedding day, I found that shit out." Laura then turns back to glare at her mother and Shayla looks at me. I wait to see if she's going to say anything.

"What was the thing you found out that you couldn't forgive?" Luca quietly asks.

I brace myself, knowing that what I'm about to tell them is going to fucking kill them and decide to just go for it, do it fast. Like ripping off a band-aid. "You guys, ain't my kids."

With that Shayla starts her bawling, and I roll my eyes.

"Your Uncle Matt is your father. That's why I left. I couldn't do it. I couldn't stay here, knowing you weren't mine, knowing what my brother did to my family, and his." Laura cries, Luca doesn't look as angry with me as before. "I'm sorry kids, I was willing to leave this all a lie, but I can't. I need my woman back, but I need to fix everything first. She thinks I have kids, you guys, and that I just left you, not caring."

"But you did leave. You still abandoned us!" Luca snaps.

"I saw you, trust me. I just didn't ever approach, it hurt too much. I know me leaving and not contacting you again was a shit thing to do, but it was something I had to do. I had to get away from the hurt and anger I felt towards your mother, and you kids. I didn't want to leave you guys, but at the time it felt like the only option I had. I was never going to be out of your lives forever. Work has been my top priority, and I couldn't just leave a job to check in."

"But mom said you could have, that you had plenty of time to see us or call us, you're only a bouncer at a bar," Luca says, looking confused.

I give him a small smile. "Thing is, I'm not a bouncer, or any of the other jobs over the years I said I had, I'm a cop. Have been since before I married your mother, and a damn good undercover one too. I was never allowed to reveal that in case of my cover being blown."

Shayla snaps her eyes in my direction. *"What the hell?"* I raise a brow at her, and her dark skin pales. "You're going after Matt, aren't you?" she whispers. "That's why you told the kids the truth." She's partly right.

I nod. "My team is on their way to his offices now. I already called Layla and asked her to meet me in an hour and to turn her phone off. I want to be the one to tell her how Matt and you destroyed her life."

Her face is so pale, and she's shaking so violently, I almost feel as if I should back away in case she barfs.

"So," Luca speaks up after a few minutes. "Does that mean we have to call you Uncle Dray now?" he asks, looking disgusted.

I give him a small grin. "Yeah, kid." I pull out my phone, bringing up a picture of Melissa and our daughter Mikayla, and hand it to the kids. "That's my woman and kid."

I watch the kids scroll through the photos and smile, Luca laughs when he comes to the picture of me covered in baby shit that Melissa snapped before helping me out.

I glance back to Shayla who looks angry and upset. I pull the papers out of my coat and hand them over to her. "Sign them, now. I will be filing them myself today after I leave here, and we'll finally be done. Only reason I'm letting you keep the house is because the kids don't need to be on the street. With my brother without a job, cash, and in jail, you won't have money, so I suggest you get a job."

"I'm not signing those. Yes, I screwed up by sleeping with Matt, but I love you, I've always loved you. You were my first." I roll my eyes at her begging and even notice the kids staring at her as if she's got a screw loose.

I shrug. "Don't give a shit. You sign those, or I'll make sure you're arrested along with Matt." I lean in close. "I know you were part of some of his shit, but I left you out so the kids wouldn't be left with no one," I whisper.

She gulps, signs the papers, and hands them back.

Once Laura and Luca hand me back my phone, we say goodbyes, and I promise we will keep in touch this time. I walk out and get in my car. That was hard, but I finally don't feel like such a dick for just taking off anymore.

Chapter 7

Dray

When I walk into Chili's, I spot Layla sitting with a glass of wine at a back booth. I walk over and sit across from her, giving her a slight scare. Layla isn't as dark skinned as her cousin is. She's also ten years older than Shayla, but you wouldn't know that, only because Layla actually takes pride in herself. Today she has on a dark blonde wig. I don't understand why she won't leave the house with her natural hair. She always just says the frizzy mess she has isn't suitable.

"Shoot, Dray, I didn't even notice you were here yet, scared me," she says with a small laugh, holding her hand on her chest. "I ordered for you. Told the waitress to bring your drink when you arrived and in about ten minutes' food should be out."

"Thanks," I tell her. "Where's your kids?"

"With my parents for the day." She goes quiet for a minute. "Can I ask what this is about? You know I've always cared for you, I hated that you and Matt were no longer close."

"Can we start eating first, then I'll fill you in?" I just know if we talk before finishing our food, that there is a possibility neither of us will want to eat, especially since I'm about to flip her world upside down.

She nods and seconds later the waitress brings out our food. I finish way before she does, so I start in.

"Not sure what you know exactly about my line of work. But I'm a cop. A damn good undercover one, too."

Layla's eyes bug wide. "Really? I always thought you flitted around to just any job without really caring." She winces when that comes out of her mouth. "I'm sorry, I didn't mean to sound snotty about that."

I wave her off. "Do you even know why I left Shayla?"

"My cousin never really said much, just that you got tired of having a ball and chain around your neck and didn't want to live the monogamous life."

I shake my head in disgust. "She cheated on me. Laura and Luca aren't mine."

Her hands fly to her mouth. "What? How did you find out? I can't believe this."

"Saw it with my own eyes, I was willing to forgive it, but then when Laura was in the hospital for that infection she had? I wasn't a match. Matt was, he gave her a kidney. Got me thinking so I went and did a DNA test. She wasn't mine, neither was Luca. I couldn't forgive that, ever. So, I left." Took me a good month to put it together. At first, I was thankful to Matt for saving my daughter, didn't even pay attention after Shayla and I were proven not to be a match, but then after knowing that Shayla cheated on me once, the pieces of how Matt could be a match became clear.

"Who?"

I grab her hand and rub the top of it.

"Please no," she whimpers, as if she knows who I'm going to say.

"I'm sorry."

"Fifteen years I've wasted on that ass, and he was cheating the whole time, wasn't he?" She asks me, the hurt and anger clear in her voice. I don't really know what more to say to her about this, so I grab some papers out of my jacket, hand them to her and continue, "That's everything I have on Matt. As we speak, he's being arrested. I wanted to be the one to tell you this, not have you find out from the raid."

Tears fall down her face. "I'm sorry, Dray. I should have known all this. I should have seen it. How can I be so stupid?"

I get out of my seat and go to her side, pulling her in for a hug. "Not your fault. I'm the ass that let it go on this long myself." I let her cry onto my shirt.

"Well look at this. Melissa dumped you at the altar because you had a wife, and now you're with someone else. Didn't take you long, did it, you fuck face?" I look up to see Cori glaring down at me.

I clench my jaw. I always liked Cori, and she always liked me, but now she hates me more than she seems to hate her own mother. "It's not what you think."

Cori snorts. "Bullshit, you're nothing but a whore. I'm glad Melissa is gone, miss her like hell, but if this is what you're doing, I'm glad she and Mikayla are away from you."

I gently move Layla and stand up, grabbing Cori by the arm. "What do you mean she's gone?" I ask, panicked. She can't be gone. I need her.

She throws my hand off and glares. "Just what I said, dipshit. Gone. G-O-N-E *Gone*. And if her father has a say in it, you'll never get near her again." With that she gives me an evil smirk and walks away, carrying bags of takeout.

I run after her but she's quick. She gets into Blake's car and they take off the second they see me jogging toward them. I yell at them to stop but knowing they won't, I finally give up.

I walk back into the restaurant and sit back down, my head in my hands. *"Fuck!"* I snarl. If she went with Hangman, I'll never be able to get close to her.

"You have a child?" Layla asks. I almost forgot about her.

I nod. "Yeah. I was about to get married to the love of my life, and then Shayla walks in screaming about how we're still married." She's about to say something when I cut her off. "Do you have a place to stay?"

She nods. "Of course. My parents will let us stay with them for as long as we need." She gives me a smirk, "I had a feeling he was doing something shady for a long time, but I put it off, because I'm a woman. You know women can be irrational, looks like I didn't have any reason to be, should have followed my gut." I reach across the table, giving her hand a squeeze as she continues. "I'll be taking Matt to the cleaners. And now all his money and companies will be mine, since I have proof of infidelity plus the prenup he signed. Since my father gave him all his start up, well, that ass will be homeless." She gives me a wink with that.

Shit, this isn't good for Laura and Luca. They'll have nothing, especially since Shayla is too lazy to work.

"I'll be talking to Shayla, too."

"About what?"

"About having the kids come live with me. I'll give her a nice big cheque, and I know she'll hand them over. They'll have a loving home with me. I can't fault them for being my bastard of a husband's children."

There goes my worry. I know Layla and her family will take good care of those kids. She's a better person than I am. I left because I couldn't see at them everyday, not when every time I looked at them, I saw my brother staring back at me.

"You can keep all those papers; they may help you fast track the divorce."

I give her a hug, tell her to keep in touch and head home, calling my boss again.

"Spurl."

"Dray again. Forget sending me to a different department, I want a transfer to the Saint John Police Force the minute you can make it happen." I click off before he can respond. Do I want to move to the other side of the country? No, but Melissa is there with my daughter. I have no fuckin' clue how long it will take me to win her back, and if she ends up wanting to stay there? Well, I'd do anything for her. Even live in a shit city.

Chapter 8

Melissa

Cori texted me a picture of Dray with his arms wrapped around another woman. A woman I didn't recognize, and she was not his wife. "He sure gets around," I mutter, tears forming in my eyes.

I hear Mikayla shouting in her room, "Up. Up. Up." Wiping the tears that leaked out, I go and get her up, changing her diaper and playing with her on the floor.

"Want to watch *Frozen*, baby girl?" I ask her, smiling. She's addicted to that movie and I can't seem to get her to watch anything else. The damn movie is on repeat almost every day, and it's doing my head in, but it keeps her happy. The only time I actually enjoyed this movie was the first time I watched it, and then just the other day when I caught my father singing along with Mikayla when he didn't realize I was done with my shower. He tried to be big scary biker dude with me, threatening me not to say a word, but I just laughed in his face. It's something I might not let him live down.

She grins and screams, "Elsa!"

I chuckle. "Okay, baby, let's go put it on."

Getting her set up in the living room with Frozen blasting away, I go into the kitchen to tidy up. Carson told me not to worry about the mess, that he'd get people over later to clean the place, but I may as well do something with my time.

I start thinking back on the times Dray and I had. Maybe I should have just resisted him more. If I had, I probably wouldn't be feeling the way I do now.

When he found out I was pregnant, he was there every single day trying to make things up to me. He just kept saying his headspace was fucked up and he wasn't thinking properly the night we were together. He honestly didn't even remember being with me.

When he first told me that, it killed me. I'd finally given into him and he had fucked me brutally and beautifully. I never would have thought he was drunk, sure didn't seem or act like it. When it was done and over, after the best orgasm I've ever had, he walked out without looking back. That hurt, I ended up going back out to the bar and getting pukey drunk, something that has never happened to me in my life. I never got hangovers or got sick from drinking too much, but that night I did.

As I was leaving I heard noises coming from the back alley, where we had just been hours before, and that's where I saw him. Screwing some blonde bitch, the same way he did me. I knew at that moment I would hate him forever.

Then weeks later my fears were revealed. I was pregnant with his child. Blake, my brother-in law went over and apparently had a chat with Dray, because the very next day, Dray was banging on my door demanding to speak with me. I've never seen a man apologize so much in my life, but he did it. I'd like to say I forgave him at that moment, but I didn't.

I held a grudge. Sure, I let him come to all the doctors' visits and ultrasound appointments with me, even let him buy me supper a few times at his insistence, of course. But I didn't budge. I barely spoke to him. I was still so deeply hurt.

Then my hormones got the best of me and I forgave him. It was the two of us from that day out, until my wedding day of course.

Snapping back to reality, I realize I let the sink overflow and try to quickly get it cleaned up. Once everything is spotless, my phone chimes with a text.

Don't wait up. – Dad

I don't know how to feel about this because I don't know him. Should I refer to him as my dad or Carson? Would it be weird for me to flat out ask him what he wants me to call him?

Maybe I should just let it come naturally, whatever feels right at the time.

It took Cori a few months before she finally started calling Sam her dad.

**

I've finally got the house cleaned and put Mikayla down for the night after reading her two stories, so I decide to explore more of the house and see what the backyard is like.

I go downstairs to the basement, since when I walked in it looked like it was unfinished, but surprisingly, it's just a giant man cave.

Pool table, check.

The biggest TV I've ever seen, check.

A fully decked out bar, check.

I wonder if he has the boys over often enough to use this stuff?

I see two doors off to the side and look in the first one, full bathroom. Nothing interesting. Basic. The other room is a giant laundry room. Don't think I've ever seen one this big before, two washers, two dryers, a huge sink in the middle. What on earth does he need all that for? I'll have to ask him later. I also notice there is a huge chest freezer and a stand-up freezer in this space too. I'm hesitant to open them, in case I find something I shouldn't. Dead body, maybe? Opening the chest freezer hesitantly, I let out a sigh of relief when it's just filled with food. Mostly bread, French fries and freezer meals. Shutting it I open the stand-up freezer, and see it's filled full of meat. All in ziplocked freezer bags. Steaks, Roasts, stew meat, chicken upon chicken, *hell,* different kinds of pig too. He must buy from farms and cut this himself.

I know Moira does this, said it's cheaper, but I didn't think someone like Carson would do this.

I turn off the lights and head back upstairs to check out the yard. To say I'm shocked would be an understatement. Tori never told me how huge this place was. The backyard could easily fit another house in it. Looking over the huge deck he has, there is tons of grass space, even a playground that looks new, and a huge pool with a connecting hot tub. Hmm, I'm gonna have to talk to him about that, a fence is going to need to go up, so Mikayla is safe.

As I go back inside, I hear the doorbell go off. Frowning, I look at the time and see that's it's just after nine at night. Who could that be?

I smile politely when I open the door and the extremely skinny, pinchy faced, blonde woman standing there gives me a once over and then sneers. "What are you doin' in *my* man's house?" she demands.

"Um, excuse me?"

"You heard me, *bitch,*" she shouts. This woman is insane.

"Could you please lower your voice, my daughter is sleeping."

"*Daughter*? That bastard got you knocked up? He just scrapped his bitch wife off, he's supposed to be mine now." She tries to get up in my face and I shove her back.

"Look, my dad isn't home right now, but I can tell him you stopped by. Also, never ever, call Tori a bitch again, *ever.* She's one of the best women I know, so you shut your mouth!" I snap.

She backs up, looking surprised. "You're dad? I thought this was Hangman's house."

I roll my eyes. "It is, and he's not here right now. So please leave."

"Tell him April stopped by. We need to talk."

This bitch, seriously?

"If he wants to see you, he'll go to you, don't come back here." I slam the door in her face and lock it.

No wonder Tori left him if those are the types of women he bangs.

Flashback Chapter

First meet

Melissa

I've snuck into this club many times with friends, my sister Cori, or men I'm out on dates with. At first it wasn't much of a thing for me, have a few drinks, dance, then leave. But a month ago, a new bouncer was added to the place. He goes by Monster, I can see why. Huge hulking black man that looks scary as hell. But damn if my panties don't get soaked every single time I look at him.

Sure, I might have found myself a crushing on the guy, but I don't think he likes me much. Every time I try to flirt with him, all he does is glare at me. Well, at least the last time he saw me anyways, the other few times he looked at me as if he wanted to eat me.

As I'm dancing with Morgan, a friend from school, a hand comes down on my arm. I'm spun around and stare up into the face of Monster. Shit, he looks furious.

"Can I help you?" I yell over the music.

"Yeah, you can get the fuck out."

Narrowing my eyes, I return his daggered glare. "And why would I do that?"

"Because you're under age. Fuckin' Jailbait. We don't need this place shut down."

Damn, I knew I would probably get caught for this at some point. Randy, the owner of this bar, most likely figured it out, since he's been screwing my sister on and off for a while.

"Legal age next week, dick head. What's the big deal?" I argue, trying to throw his arm off me, but he's not budging. I try to make him leave me alone, but he's not having it, and he's obviously too strong for me to fight off, so I give in, letting him drag me through the club and out the back door.

I look behind me before the door shuts and don't see Morgan following, that bitch.

"Don't come back until you are actually eighteen," Monster says, towering over me.

"Oh, fuck you. Randy doesn't care. He's banging my sister."

He steps further into my space, and I stand my ground. "He does care, why do you think it's me dragging you out and not him? He doesn't wanna piss off your sister."

He's so close, I can practically feel his lips on my face as he talks so near to my mouth. Obviously, I'm not thinking straight, because one minute he's giving me a long ass lecture, then the next, I'm grabbing him and kissing him with all I have. He's big, scary, and oh so damn sexy.

His hands go around me, to my waist, then move to my ass, giving me a squeeze. As his tongue touches mine. I moan, oh god, he's an amazing kisser. But my moan must have snapped him back into reality, because now I'm being shoved away.

"Fuck!" he hollers. "That shouldn't have happened. You're fucking seventeen, jailbait."

He doesn't bother to look at me as he goes back into the club, leaving me standing outside alone.

Maybe I'm not the only one with a crush after-all. I rub my lips still feeling his kiss.

Chapter 9

Dray

I pull up to my brother's offices and notice that almost every officer on the force is here. Everyone is coming out with their arms loaded with boxes, probably all the paperwork that's in there. As soon as I see Matt being led out in cuffs, I get out of my truck and slam the door shut, leaning against it.

He sees me and his eyes narrow. I give him a smug grin and open my jacket, so he can see my badge.

He yells, "*You son of a bitch! You did this!*"

"Sure did," I say with a shrug.

"You won't find shit! This is just revenge because I fucked your wife and fathered the kids you thought were yours." He sneers as the cops holding him bring him closer.

"Better watch what you say. Monster here is a good buddy of ours and our team leader. We would be more than happy to look the other way if he decided to break your neck right here," Locke states, using my nickname and giving me a wink.

They start to put him into their cruiser when I lean down so he can see my face. "Layla knows everything now, just so you know. All the women, the other kids you fathered, all of it. She'll be ruining you more than I already have," I pause and grin. "You have a good day now and don't drop the soap."

Locke and Stax chuckle as the door gets shut. Matt looks pissed as he shouts and kicks at the door.

"Captain says he's going to be held without any bail possibilities. Also, be on the lookout for an angry black woman because she'll be filing for divorce first thing in the morning. If you could help her out to speed the process up, that would be the best thing ever," I tell them and walk away. As I get to my truck, I pause and turn back. "Place an anonymous call into CPS, tell them to head over to Shayla's." I was gonna leave the kids with Shayla, leave her out of this, but now I'm handing over everything I have with her name on it, too. "Already talked to Matt's wife, Layla, her cousin. She is more than happy to have custody of those kids." I hand him the folder I kept out of this investigation, everything they'll need to lock Shayla up is in it.

They both nod and Locke looks as if he's in his glory, he hates Shayla almost more than I ever did.

"Where you off to now?" Stax asks.

"I'm going to make sure the divorce goes through then I'm going to get back my woman and kid." I slam my truck door closed as I hop in and start it up.

I'm going to get Melissa back, and I don't care how dirty I must play to win.

**

I pull into the Angels Warriors compound and get out. I see the men coming outside instantly, all glaring at me. I have a feeling before I can say what I need to say, they'll want to get in a few punches, and I don't blame them.

"We need to talk."

"Fuckin' right we do, but we also have the right to kick your fuckin' face in before that!" Reaper shouts at me.

"Calm down, Reaper, we'll hear him out, and if we don't like what he has to say, we'll let you at him," Angel says calmly, still glaring at me, being the voice of reason.

I notice Trevor isn't with the guys, but I wasn't expecting him. Since he has Tori back, he's probably not left her side once. The guy was torn apart for months when Tori left him, just like I'm feeling now.

I follow them inside and take a seat at the table in the common room, furthest away from them, so I can say everything I need to without a random fist in my face.

"My name is Drayton Jacob Hante, I'm an undercover police officer for the Red Deer police." At this announcement all the men look shocked as fuck. Obviously, they already knew my name. "I've been undercover for years, never once have been ousted. I worked as a bouncer, as you know, to help take down a drug ring. Not even my ex-wife knew I was a cop. Thought I was a low life who just worked shitty jobs wherever I could."

At the mention of Shayla, they all go back to glaring at me.

"I divorced Shayla years ago, except I found out I was lied to, and a false divorce decree was mailed to me instead of her actually filing the damn papers. I'm not a deadbeat dad. They aren't my kids. The bitch cheated on me, but I forgave her, until the girl I thought was my daughter almost died. It came out that both my children were fathered by my brother. As soon as I knew that, I left and never went back. Yes, it's still shitty of me to have left two small kids the way I did. But I couldn't be around them because it killed me too much. At the time they were too young to understand that I wasn't their father."

I take a breath, as the air in the room settles. "I love Melissa, she's the love of my life. She thinks all this awful shit about me, and I get it, I could have at least told her about

Shayla and the kids, but it was a hurt I didn't want to dredge up. And until last month, I couldn't say anything about my real job because I was still undercover at the club. I couldn't risk my cover being blown. But now I don't give a shit. I told my boss I was done with undercover, if it means letting Melissa have and know all of me, it's what I gotta do."

"Fuck, man, you could have told us," Zippo shouts as he bangs his fist on the table.

"I thought about it, but could any of you have kept it to yourselves and not tell the women? The women who would have told Melissa, and then she would have told Cori, who has a huge mouth." I give them a smirk.

Gavin laughs. "He's got a point. But thing is, if Hangman finds out you're a cop…....." He trails off, shaking his head.

"I've already told my boss, anything to do with the Untamed MC I can't have a part of because the pres is my damn father-in-law. So Hangman doesn't have to worry about me in his club, I just want Melissa."

Reaper walks around the table, stopping in front of me, and his fist slams into my face. *"Fuck."* I wasn't expecting that.

"You deserved that. It was for hurting Melissa. Never should have not told her about the ex-wife shit. She would have understood it. Stop bein' a damn pussy and get her back,

I miss her around here, and now she's on the other side of the damn country. Fuck that." He hands me a slip of paper with an address on it and I smile. "You go get our girl back. Make her listen to you. Sure, she'll be pissed at first, probably won't hear you out, but you make her."

Chapter 10

Melissa

I wake up to noise in the kitchen and check the time, ten a.m. *Damn it!* I slept in. I bolt out of bed and go find Mikayla. She's not in her room. Running into the kitchen she's there, playing the drums with my dad and three other men on the floor with pots and pans.

"Uh, hi," I say, waving awkwardly.

"Thought I'd let you sleep in, but once she found these, couldn't keep the noise down," Carson tells me with a smile.

I smile. "Uh, cool. Thank you. I feel great today. I'm just going to go and get some clothes on," I say, suddenly remembering I'm only in a tee shirt and panties, and there are strange men around.

"Look at her again, your heads will be hanging on the wall inside the clubhouse, you fucks. Did you not hear what I said last night?"

"Sorry, brother, but she's hot." I hear one man say.

Then a grunt. "Fuck, man, don't punch me in the face, I need this to get into Anara's pants."

"She still turning you down?" I hear another man ask.

"Yeah." The first man grunts in response. "I should just take her the club way. Bring her in, pin her to the club fuck table, and bang her. Claimed, instantly. Done with this courting bullshit."

I freeze when I hear that. They rape women to claim as theirs? That makes me feel sick.

"Ever think she's turning you down because maybe you have a small dick?" I hear my dad ask.

I can't help the small giggle that escapes me as I head down the hall and into my room.

I quickly get dressed, just throwing on a pair of yoga pants and a tank top and go back out to the living room, where everyone has moved to.

"Got a prospect in the kitchen, he's gonna cook up some breakfast. What d'you want?" Carson asks me.

"Bacon and eggs? And I want lots of runny yolk."

He nods. "Prospect? You hear that?"

"Yeah, Pres!" gets shouted back.

"If her eggs aren't the way she wants them, you'll never get your patch."

"They will be done to her perfection."

I raise my brows at my father and shake my head. This club is so different. The Angels don't have prospects, anyone that wants in, is just in.

"I'll be in the next room with Rage, got shit to discuss. You stay here with these brothers and play with your kid." He pauses before leaving and looks at me. "The Ass on the floor is Slammer, bitch on the couch is Dirty."

He walks away, and I sit down on the couch. I turn to the man named Dirty and stare at him. I don't get it. Why is that his nickname when he's the cleanest guy I've ever met? His hands even look as if he gets manicures. Only thing that makes him look like he belongs in my dad's club is the fact he's extremely built and has tattoos all over his neck, hands, and arms.

"Why you starin'?" he asks.

"Uh, well, I was wondering. Why the name Dirty?"

"These fucks thought it would suit me, since I'm OCD about germs. Constantly washing my hands and any area I'm in, manicures all the time, manscaping, shit like that," he tells me with a shrug, not giving a shit if what he just said takes a hit to his scary vibe.

"Where do you get your mani's done? Because you do realize that nail salons are the worst places for someone that has issues about germs?"

"Yeah, we got girls at the club that can do that shit. I buy all my own stuff I keep in my room," he replies, as if this really isn't a big deal. "And my OCD isn't really that bad. I just know that other people can be nasty, and some don't wash their hands after using the bathroom. I ain't touching a fuckin' surface that could possibly have shit on it."

Huh, I can understand that. Now my thoughts are about how many surfaces shit could be on. I shudder. I turn to look at Slammer, who is on the floor getting play tickled by Mikayla. Slammer looks similar to Dirty, but his hair is long, down to his shoulders, and his short beard is all scruffy, making his hotness ten times hotter. He's also bigger than Dirty. Where on earth does my dad find these type of men? "What about you? Oh wait! I know! Slam Her!" I bust out laughing, as does Dirty.

Slammer shakes his head. "Nah girl, got that name cos I'm in the Slammer often."

"Oh, well, my version is better." I give him a wink, and he smirks at me. Damn, he's hot. If I wasn't totally and completely in love with that ass, Dray, I would totally flirt with Slammer. Or hell, even Dirty. Never Rage. He's one mean looking dude. I always thought Reaper was the scariest man I've ever known. My father and Rage have him beat by a mile. That's not to say Rage isn't a good-looking guy. To be honest, if I was into the scary look, I'd be all over it. Actually, if I was into guys double my age, I'd be all over it. But Tori told me a lot about Rage. Said if I thought Hangman was a bad man, well, he had nothing on Rage.

Thinking about Dray now, maybe flirting with other men *is* just what I need. There is that old saying 'to get over someone, get under someone new' and that's exactly what I've always done in the past. Although I never had a kid before, so this will be a little different. As long as it's string free sex, I don't see why I can't indulge.

"What about me, you wanna know how I got my name?" Rage asks, coming out from the kitchen with Hangman following behind him.

"Not really. You scare the shit out of me, so I can only imagine how you got it." I see my dad smirk.

Rage shrugs and walks off as the prospect who was making breakfast comes in with my food. I look at the plate and smile, and quickly mouth a thank you as I shove the food in my mouth.

"Guy is full of rage and goes off over the littlest shit, that's how he got his name," my dad tells me, looking amused as I finish stuffing all the food on my plate in my mouth.

"What?" It comes out more like 'wah' since my mouth is full.

The guys all laugh and shake their heads. "I take it the food was good?" The prospect asks.

"Yeah, it was perfect."

"I could tell, you barely chewed."

I feel my face heating up, and I shrug, "When you have kids you have to eat as fast as possible, it's really the only way you'll get to eat."

He takes my plate from me and quickly goes back to the kitchen, I assume to clean up.

I look to my dad and get back on the topic of the nicknames. "I don't even want to know how you got yours, because I'm thinking it's something sexual, like I thought Slammer's was." I shudder at the thought. *Gross.*

"You'd be wrong then. My favorite way to end someone is to hang them as I watch them bleed to death."

He stomps off, and I'm left staring at his retreating back. "Please tell me he didn't just say that to me. He knows who

61

I'm related to and who my family is, right? I don't want to know that shit," I whisper frantically to Dirty.

"Don't worry about it, kid, he wouldn't have said that shit to you if he didn't think he could trust you. Seems to want you in his life so he won't hold anything back from ya."

That's kind of what I was afraid of. This whole club is just so different from the club I grew up in, everything said or done here is a shock to me. I'm not sure I'll ever get used to it.

"*OH!*" I stand up and go to find my dad. "Um, forgot to tell you earlier, a woman named April stopped by last night." I wrinkle my nose.

His face goes hard. "What the fuck was that bitch here for?"

"I don't know. At first she thought I was with you, so she got all pissy about me being in her man's house, but eww, no. You're old and my dad."

"Watch it kid. I'm not that old, and if you see that bitch again, don't talk to her. Just shut the door and lock it. She's not supposed to be here. She knows better, now she's asking for trouble."

Uh oh, maybe I should have kept my mouth shut. I take a step back from him and he glares at me.

"Go back and see to your kid, the guys will stay with you. I have some shit to take care of." He stomps passed me, and I hear him slam the front door. Whoever that April girl was, she seems to be in some deep shit. *Yikes.*

Chapter 11

Hangman

Why I ever fucked that bitch, I'll never know. She was easy pussy, that was that. I make it to April's house and check the time, just after one, good, Emily is still at school.

I don't bother knocking and walk right in. I see her at the sink, washing dishes, so she doesn't know I'm here yet. Stupid bitch. Ever since I sent Tori back to my brother, divorce finalized, April got it in her head that I would be with her now, thinking I only stayed away from her because of Tori. I never touched April again, not after I fucked her at a club party and got her knocked up. You'd think after not taking her back to my bed after eight years, she'd get a fuckin' clue.

I grab her by the back of her neck and squeeze as I turn her around to face me.

Her hand goes over her heart. "Holy shit, you scared me." I must have been drunk as fuck when I banged this bitch, she's not even that hot. Blonde hair to her shoulders, and she's skinny. I usually stay away from the skinny bitches, bones hurt when tryin' to fuck.

"Why were you at my house last night?"

"I wanted to see you, baby," she says, trying to sound sexy. Instead she sounds like a whiny two-year-old brat that has a plugged-up nose.

"We're not together, we're never gonna be together, what the fuck is your problem?" I sneer in her face.

Her eyes narrow on me. "That's bullshit, Hangman. We have a kid together. We only didn't get married because you were married to that stupid bitch." With those words and my hand still on her neck, I slam her face into the countertop. Blood instantly spurts out of her nose.

She screams and cries.

"Shut the fuck up," I growl into her face when I pull her back up from the counter and wrap a hand around her neck. I squeeze and watch as she struggles to breathe, fuck this shit is getting me hard. May as well give this bitch what she wants, since I need a release.

Stepping away from her, I rip her blouse open, the buttons popping and falling to the ground, she has nice tits at least. I cup one. "You want this? This what you wanted?" I twist her nipple.

"Yes, please." She moans.

"Clothes off, turn around." She obeys instantly, once her clothes are off, she leans over the counter, not seeming to give a shit she's still covered in blood, as is the counter she's leaning over. Grabbing a condom our of my back pocket, I rip it open, while using one hand to pull my jeans down a bit. Once covered, I grab her hair and line my dick up with her cunt.

"Beg me," I demand.

"Please, Hangman, fuck me. I need it."

"Then you'll get it bitch," I say as I slam inside of her. Her pussy isn't that great, but she'll do for a fast fuck.

"Fuck yes!" she screams out as I pound into her, faster and harder as I feel my cock swelling up, getting ready to let go. I pull out, and she cries out. "No, I still need it."

"On your knees." I take off the condom and shove it into her mouth, she gags as I hit the back of her throat, fuck yeah, I could kill her like this. Be hot as fuck way to go.

As I'm about to cum, I shove her head off my cock and fist it, "Fuck yeah." I grunt as I shoot my spunk all over her face.

She looks up at me stunned as I tuck my cock back into my pants. I lean over her, staring into her ugly fucking cum covered face, nose still bleeding. "Victoria was a good woman that I did wrong. She was way too fuckin' good for me. With her gone, it means shit for you. The arrangement stays the same. You come near me one more time, or my other daughter and grandkid, I'll kill you like I wanted to the first time you threatened me."

She shakes in fear and nods. You'd think this bitch would be smart enough to try and at least wipe that shit off her face as I'm talking to her.

"Good. I don't want your fuckin' pussy again. Hell, I don't even remember having it the first time, so you obviously weren't any fuckin' good in the first place and even just now, you were fuckin' shit. Had to choke you to even cum." She takes in a shaky breath and backs away from me as I spit on her face. "I want Emily this weekend, she's gonna meet her big sister. I'll have a prospect come to pick her up, because as of now, I never see you, you get me? That fuck, you better have enjoyed it because it's the last you'll get out of me"

"Yes, Hangman. I get you," she whispers.

"Good." I walk out of her house, get back on my bike, and head back to my house.

Chapter 12

Slammer

When I saw Melissa coming out of her room this morning, I instantly knew she was mine. The way her tee barely covered the tops of her thighs, teasing at her panties. I was fucking hard. Then she came back wearing these tight pants that hugged her ass. She was driving me wild. I know she has issues, but I don't care. Something inside me just snapped, and I felt a burning need to claim her, to make her mine. To plant my baby inside her. I've never been faithful to a woman a day in my life, but with her, I feel it, the feeling inside me that I could never be with anyone but her.

I can picture myself at her side helping her raise her kid. I've never wanted that before. *Fuck*, I run the other way when a bitch mentions having a kid but there is something about Melissa.

The way she smiled at me, with her sexy little smirk, the way she blushed when I spoke to her … *goddamn,* I want her.

Now to convince Hangman I'm good enough for her, even good enough to be a father to her kid, and convince her Dray isn't the one for her.

As Melissa plays with her daughter on the floor, Dirty takes me aside. "Brother, I saw the way you looked at Pres' kid. Bitch is hot as hell, but not worth Hangman's knife."

I shake my head. "I'll deal with it."

He pokes a finger in my chest. "Were you not there when Hangman told the club that no one touches her? That includes you."

I grab his finger and twist it back. "Brother, I said I'll deal with it, and he didn't say no one touches her, he said no one touches her *unless* they can treat her good and could be a good father to Mikayla."

His brows raise with a smug grin. "And you think that's you? Sorry to say it man, but you aren't the settlin' type. You have a different bitch, sometimes two, in every city we visit. Fuck, seein' you as a dad, that's hilarious, you are not dad material."

"Not anymore I won't," I vow, more to myself than Dirty.

"The fuck, man? You're turnin' into a pussy." He shakes his head. "A one-woman man, my ass. I'll believe it when I see it. You know even Hangman doesn't do the whole one-woman thing, but he wants that for his kid and grandkid. Think about that. You and I both know you can't do that."

I want to punch him right in the face. "*Fuck, Dirty. No woman has ever made me want to be faithful, the right woman though, I would be for her.*" I shove him away from me and walk back to the living room to play with the girls. Family man. *I can do this.* Now to figure out how to get Melissa to stop having feelings for her baby daddy.

I'll do whatever it takes to make her mine.

Squatting down in the floor, I pick up a few of the blocks. "What are you building?"

The little girl stares up at me with wide eyes and grins. She has her mother's smile, but she must have her father's eyes, along with his skin color because Melissa is as white as a ghost, and this beautiful little girl is a milk chocolate color.

As I play with the kid, I watch Melissa talking with Dirty, making me feel like a jealous fuckwad.

"So, you grew up with the Angels, huh?" he asks her.

Her smile lights up the whole room, and I feel my pulse quicken.

"Yup, those people are my family, they're the best family anyone could ever have."

"Fuck that shit, they ain't nothin' but a bunch of fuckin' pansy assed pussies," Rage puts in.

Melissa's head twists so hard, I'm worried about an exorcist moment happening, and I grab her hand, which feels fucking amazing in mine. "Let it go."

She sits back down, but still glares at Rage. "The Angels Warriors are my family. They saved my sister and me. They raised us, put us through school, bought us both our first cars. They took care of us, loved us. You will never, and I mean *never*, say nasty shit about them *ever* again around me. If you do, I don't give a flying fuck that you're scary as hell, I'll slice your dick off and shove it up your ass."

"Fuck this shit." Rage gets up looking pissed as fuck and stomps out of the room, slamming the back door.

"Wow, no one has ever spoken like that to him before, at least none that are still alive," Dirty tells her. "Just be careful around him, though. You most likely will get away with a lot of shit because Hangman is your dad, but Rage has his name for a reason."

He's right about that, during her rant at Rage, both Dirty and I were getting ready to brace in case we had to stop him from killing her. I've seen him lose his temper over less things than a woman back talking him.

Chapter 13

Melissa

Carson wasn't gone long, although when he came back he was pissy. I just avoided him and did my own thing. Dirty and Slammer left not long after he came back, but Rage was still here. The guy is creepy. Sure he's hot for a guy almost my dads age, but his scare factor cancels out that hotness. Slammer and Dirty seemed nice. They talked to me about life, mine and theirs, and they seemed interested in the Angels Warriors.

When we started talking about the club, Rage put a stop to it, saying something about the Angels being a pussy club, which pissed me off. I was about to get up and punch him, but Slammer told me to let it go. But I didn't, sort of. I didn't hit him, but I did tell him that they were my family, and if he spoke about them like that again around me, I'd slice his dick off. Dirty thought that was hilarious, said no one has ever spoken like that to Rage, ever, and lived to tell the tale.

Rage stomped out of the room and went outside for a smoke. It was then that Dirty informed me that I should watch

72

myself around him, if I was anyone else, and not Hangman's kid, he would have put a bullet in my head for speaking to him that way.

Now I'm sitting on the couch flicking through the channels while Mikayla naps, bored out of my mind. Carson, Dad, Hangman--whatever the hell--comes and takes a seat beside me and I hear the front door close. Good, Rage is leaving.

"You're gonna meet my other kid this weekend. Her name's Emily. She's seven."

My eyes widen. "Wow, never been a big sister before." His eyes crinkle, and I decide to ask him a stupid question. "Um, what does she call you? Is there something you want me to call you?" I swear I feel and sound like a moron asking this.

"Whatever you are comfortable with. Carson, Hangman, Dad, whatever. Emily calls me dad, although she does fuck up and call me Hangman sometimes, since for years I didn't allow her to know me as her father. Didn't want anyone but my club to know, in case that shit got out to Tori. She's a good kid, but her mom's a cunt. But don't worry, you won't see her again. I've made sure of that."

I can feel the blood draining from my face. Does that mean he killed her?

"I didn't kill the bitch so get that look off your face. I wanted to, but then I'd have to have Emily full time, and that's not something I wanna do. Love the kid but losing Tori because of her…." he trails off, shaking his head. "I know it ain't her fault, it's mine, but still."

I reach out and grab his hand, giving him a squeeze. "You really did love Tori, didn't you?"

"Yeah, but not in the right way, not the way she should've been loved. *Fuck*, I sound like a pussy. When the kid wakes up, get her dressed and shit, we're gonna go out for supper." He gets up and stomps to his room.

I chuckle quietly. He is always stomping. Can't he just walk like a normal person?

I get up and walk to my room. Mikayla will be up soon, so I may as well get ready first. I grab a pair of blue jeans and tee shirt, then I plug my straightener in so I can fix my hair. When I'm finished, I hear Mikayla call out for me. But I'm not quick enough, as I open my bedroom door, I see dad stomping into her room and picking her up.

Again, he surprises me. "I'll change her, you can grab your coat and shit and wait by the door."

Minutes later we're in his truck and take off. The ride is quiet, except for Mikayla babbling in the back seat.

We pull into a parking lot and I look at the building in front of us. *Deluxe*. That's an odd name for a restaurant.

"It's not fancy, but they have the best fish and chips around." I shrug, I wouldn't know, we don't have this place out west. But I'll take his word for it.

"At some point, I want to try out some pizza place called *Greco*. Tori talked about it many times, said it was the best pizza in the world, and she can't find a place in Alberta that even comes close to its goodness."

He chuckles. "We'll order that this weekend when Emily is with us."

I smile at him and get out, going to the back to get Mikayla. "Wan Papa," she says, holding her arms out around me to him.

He smiles and takes her instantly.

As we step inside, the place goes quiet. I see some people look scared. Others look shocked to see him carrying around a toddler.

"Go find a seat, I'll grab a highchair," he tells me. I nod and slide into the first booth I see that's empty. As I take off my jacket and set it beside me, he comes back and plunks Mikayla right in the seat.

The whole time he's doing this, people are still staring. "Um, everyone is looking at us."

His head snaps up from Mikayla, and he glares around the room. "The fuck you starin' at? I'm here with my kid and grandkid, now fuck off and look somewhere else before I decide to fuck with ya's," he announces. Everyone immediately turns away. "Fuckin' nosey asswipes. You know what you want or want me to surprise ya?"

"Do they have poutine here? I'd like that for sure, and some battered fish?"

"Be back," he says and takes off to the registers and places our order. Occasionally, I notice people glancing but thankfully no one is outright looking at us anymore.

Chapter 14

Slammer

"Yo, Slammer, you want in on this action?" Dirty calls as he ploughs into the snatch on the pool table.

"Nah, I'm good." Normally I'd be all up in the bitch, no hesitation, but after meeting Melissa I don't want another woman touching me. Watching the bitch Dirty is fuckin' moan usually gets me instantly hard, but nothing. I look down and growl at my dick, "Fucking broken piece of shit."

"Dude, you talkin' to your dick?" Rage asks, his brows raised.

"Fuck off."

"Haven't seen you bang a club whore in a while, not since Hangman's kid showed up. You want her?"

I grunt, rubbing my face. "Yeah."

"I'm not one for this pussy talk, but Hangman will gut you if you hurt her. You've never been faithful to any of the bitches you've been with, and a woman like Melissa, you have to be faithful."

"I know that, and that's not the problem." Melissa would be worth my dick never fucking another bitch until the day I died. "The problem is she still loves that fucker Dray. I want her. Want her so bad, I feel the urge to grab her, and fuck her raw, getting her pregnant. So bad, Rage, I feel possessed with the need."

"*Well fuck.*" He hands me a bottle of liquor from behind the bar.

Fuck is right.

"I'm gonna make her mine. Show her what a real man is about." I shake my head and hand the bottle back to him. If I want Melissa, I gotta keep my head on straight.

I gotta show her I can step up to the plate and be the man her and her daughter need.

Chapter 15

Melissa

One Month Later

As I finish cleaning, I hear Dad's bike coming down the street. Good thing I finished, otherwise he'd probably yell at me again. He keeps telling me to fuck off with cleaning his house, that he's got people that do that, but I can't just sit around doing nothing.

Every other weekend I get to see my little sister, Emily. To say she's adorable is an understatement. She looks so much like I did as a kid. How that woman April made such a beauty is beyond me. Dad also is devoted to her, and every weekend when it's time for her to go back to her mom's, she gets quiet. I hate that for her. Next weekend I promised Emily I'd take her and Mikayla out to the rec center for a swim, and her eyes lit right up.

"Kid!" he shouts as he opens his front door.

"Yes, your majesty? You called," I sass him.

His eyes narrow on me, but his lips twitch. "Fuckin' smartass." He shakes his head and digs something out of his pocket. "Got you somethin'."

"What now? You are always getting me something. You have to stop." Just last week he came home with a brand-new car for me and a new car seat. I get he's trying to make up for twenty years of not being around, but it wasn't his fault.

"Just shut up and accept it. I bought you a building. It'll take four to six months for all the renovations, you just gotta approve the plans for what you want and think of a name."

"You bought me a building? Think of a name? What?" I ask, confused.

"Your restaurant. You're a fuckin' good cook, and you told me yourself your dream is to run your own place, so I'm doin' that for you. We'll go tomorrow to look at the space, you look at the plans and pick one, so the construction team can get on it."

I burst out crying. Originally my dream was to be a nurse, and I busted my ass to finish my nursing degree, but once I held that paper in my hand, the love for that line of work vanished. I felt like shit that I wasted all that money to get a nursing degree, and in the end, I realized it wasn't what I really wanted at all.

"Fuck kid, what's the matter with you?"

"Y-y-you bought me a restaurant, you bought me a car, y-y-you." I sob as he pulls me into his arms and hugs me tight.

"Love you kid, you're mine. I take care of what's mine, and I have a lot of making up for, so shut up and don't argue with me about that shit anymore. Might not a known about you, but still gonna do all I can to make sure you're livin' wild and free, baby."

"I love you too, Daddy," I whisper into his chest, and his arms tighten slightly when I call him that. "I seriously have the best Dad ever, thank you for loving me."

"It's not a hardship kid," he replies gruffly back to me and kisses the top of my head.

**

A Week Later

My phone rings as I finish getting dressed and I see that it's Cori. I smile. "Hey big sis."

"Hey, Melly, I miss you."

"I miss you too."

"Well, since we miss each other you should just come home."

I chuckle and shake my head, even though she can't see me. "Cori, I don't know. I'm actually liking it here."

"What?" she shouts at me. "You weren't supposed to stay there, you just wanted time to stop hurting. I got that, but you can't stay there. I need you here. With me. I'm due any day now, you need to come home."

"Cori, I love you, you've always looked out for me, and we'll visit, but right now, I'm happy where I am."

"Look, I need to talk to you about Dray."

"Stop, please don't. I don't want to talk about him, I'm moving on."

"You can't move on! It's not what you think, I promise, just listen."

"Cori, stop. I love you, you're my sister, but I'm not talking about Dray with you. I'll contact him, eventually, so he can have a relationship with Mikayla, but I'm done. He hurt me, I was the other woman," I tell her, tearing up.

"Melly, please just hear me out."

I hear Mikayla calling for me. "Sorry, but I can't. I have to go. Call me when you have the baby, I want pictures." I shut my phone off and toss it on my bed. Why on earth does she seem to be on Dray's side now? She's supposed to be on mine. Yeah, I get it that I've stayed away longer than I thought I would, but I'm loving the life I'm building here.

Last week, Dad took me to look at the building he bought for my restaurant. I was shocked! The place looked like a total dump, and so did the entire surrounding area. Dad saw the look on my face and laughed, reassuring me that everything would be fine. Apparently, the entire neighborhood was bought out, every single building and house would be torn down and rebuilt as something else. Supposedly there was plans for a strip mall, a few condos and even a hotel. So far, I would be the only place besides the hotel that would offer food.

Once I heard all about the plans, I became extremely happy. On a bad note, the building Dad bought was being torn down also, which means there is no way a restaurant will be up and running any time soon, especially not with all the surrounding construction that will be going on as well. Demolition starts tomorrow for the entire area. So roughly, we're looking at about seven to eight months before everything is up and running properly. That is, as long as we don't run into any issues along the way. Giving me plenty of time to pick out color schemes and how I want everything set up, as well as hire staff.

Mikayla throws a few toys at me, and I smile at her.

"Come on baby, let's go to the store," I say sweetly as I pick her up from the floor where she was playing.

**

"Hey there," a woman says, coming up to me.

Wow, she's beautiful. Curvy in all the right places, long black hair down to her ass, and skin color a permanent tan.

"Um, hi."

"I'm Anara. I've seen you around with Hangman, thought I'd introduce myself." She gives me a huge smile, so big I'm scared her face is gonna split like the Joker's.

"Dirty's woman?"

She throws her head back and laughs. "Hell no, that man is a player. Can't keep it in his pants. I want no part of that," she says with a shudder.

I laugh with her. "I've talked with him a few times, he's really into you." Maybe Dirty will stop bitching about her turning him down if I can convince her he's not that awful. The way his face lights up when he speaks about her, I think he's in love. I don't tell her as much. I don't want to scare her off him completely.

"Trust me, he could never handle me. I most likely would go to jail for murder, because I like my men into me and only me."

I give her a small smile. "I understand that. I'm the same way."

"I heard, girl. We all did." Giving me a sad smile, she rubs my shoulder. "We should totally get together sometime, plus I help out the club's Old Ladies when they need a babysitter. If you ever need someone to look after this cutie, I'll be more than happy to help out."

"Wow, that uh, sounds great. It would be nice to get out sometime." We talk for a while longer, until Mikayla starts getting cranky. We exchange numbers and she takes off with a promise to text me soon.

No wonder Dirty wants her, she reminds me of Hilary, Mason's dead first wife, and everyone loved her. She's beautiful and knows it, but not in a conceited in your face way, and she tells it like it is. Dirty would be an idiot if he finally did win Anara then fucked her over. I'd help Anara kill him.

I finish up my shopping and get my cranky pants daughter back home.

Home.

I never thought I would think of my father's place as home, but it is startling to feel like I belong.

Flashback Chapter

Melissa

Thanks For The Fuck

I still think about that kiss I shared with Monster. It's been months, but it's always on my mind. Obviously not his though, since I'm constantly seeing the bastard with a different woman glued to his lips every time I see him, which hasn't been all that often since our kiss. Have to say, it hurts.

Tonight, I'm out with one of my regular fuck buddies, enjoying a night out from having to listen to my sister and Blake get it on all the damn time. At the same time, I enjoy this game Monster and I seem to be playing. I practically fuck a guy in front of him, while he does the same with women. Tonight, he looks more than his usual pissed off too.

Wonder what his problem is.

I shrug it off as I make my way to the bar. Before I get the chance to order a drink, I'm out of my seat and whisked off to the back rooms. "What are you doing? I'm legal age now."

"Yeah, I know. Why the fuck you here with that tool?"

"Because I want a good long hard fuck tonight, that's why," I say snottily hoping my confession gets under his skin.

"No," he retorts, as his nostrils flair. Huh, was that steam?

"What do you mean no? I'm horny, I want it. You're not the boss of me."

"Fuck this." The second he says it his mouth comes crashing down on mine. I'm shocked at first. Mostly because I've been waiting months for this to happen again, but I can also taste the rum on his tongue.

His hands move to my dress, and he tugs it down slightly to free my tits. Leaning away from me he looks at them, "Fucking perfect", and starts to lick, suck, and bite them. Holy shit.

Before I know what's happening, his hands move, going under my dress.

"Shit, no underwear?" he growls into my neck.

"Didn't want panty lines," I croak out as his fingers slip inside me. Oh god. As he pumps his fingers into me, while sucking on my neck, I move my hands in between us, undoing his pants and pull out his dick.

"You want me, baby?"

"Please," I whimper on a shaky breath as he thrusts his fingers harder and deeper.

"Good."

I cry out as he pulls his fingers out of me, hating the loss, but instantly I'm filled up again. Oh god, he's so big.

As he pounds into me, he goes between sucking and biting my neck and kissing me, hard and rough. "Wanted you for so fuckin' long, hated that you were underage." He starts going harder and faster, almost as if he's angry with me. "Then I had to watch you slut around with those other fucking guys, fucking them in the bathroom here at the club. Wanted to kill them." Oh shit. He pulls back then slams into me hard almost as if he wants to punish me.

"Monster." I moan as I start to feel myself coming.

"No, you call me Dray when I'm inside you."

"Fuck." My breath hitches.

"Say my name, Melissa." He demands, as his mouth covers mine.

Seconds later I'm screaming his name, coming completely undone. Best sex I've ever had. He's ruined me.

We are both panting, as he's still got me pinned to the wall, and just as quickly as our fucking started, it's finished. He pulls out, stumbling a bit. Narrowing my eyes at him, I notice something I should have from the start. He's drunk.

"Thanks for the fuck," he mutters as he walks away, buttoning up his pants as he does so.

"What the fuck was that?" I whisper angrily to myself as I fix my dress. Once everything is covered up, I realize he didn't use a condom, now I have a huge mess going on, and it's sliding down my legs. "shit."

I quickly find a bathroom and start cleaning the mess, which takes forever because there is so damn much of it. Who the hell has that much goo?

Finally cleaned, I make my way back out to the main club area and search for Monster, or as I now know, Dray. I don't see him anywhere, but I do spot Randy, the club owner at the bar, talking with a bartender.

"Hey, you see Monster?" I ask him.

"Yeah, he just left out the back not too long ago, why you are looking for him?"

"Just forgot to say something to him is all." I push past him and make my way through the crowd to the back, as I open the back door, the same door that he shoved me out of the last time we interacted, I hear moaning, and grunting.

It's not uncommon, this shit usually is heard around the Clubs I go to. But the groaning sounds familiar and my heart rate spikes up. I can feel it pounding so hard in my chest it's as if it's gonna burst out. Walking around the corner, I see him. And some blonde. He's fucking her the same way he just did me.

Like I was nothing.

Well fuck him.

Tears sting at my eyes, but I refuse to cry.

Chapter 16

Slammer

Going down the hall to Pres's office I put my head in. "Pres, can we talk?"

He gives me a chin lift and I walk in, sitting in the chair across from his desk.

"I want to ask Melissa out."

His eyes widen in surprise. "Is this why you haven't been fuckin' any of the club girls?"

I nod.

"Well fuck me," he mutters. He narrows his eyes and leans back in his chair, grabbing his gun from his desk to aim it at me. "Only warning I'm gonna give ya, you hurt her, I find you with another bitch while you're with her, I'll kill you."

"I won't hurt her, that's a promise."

"Good, same goes for the kid. She's a package deal, brother, can't have one without the other."

"I know that, I want them both."

He looks at me in shock before lifting his chin, giving me the okay to go ahead.

"Got word that her ex might be coming this way, heard he's actually a cop. He wants her back."

I clench my fists and grind my teeth. "Well then, looks like I need to make her mine quick, so the fucker can't have her back."

"You're one of my best brothers in the club, good man, never been good to women, but you got my blessing to have Melissa, just remember what I said."

I give him a chin lift and stand up, but I turn back around as I get to the door. "Mind babysitting Mikayla tomorrow night?"

"*Fuck*." He shakes his head, his lip twitching with a smile. "I'll give Anara a call, she'll take Mikayla."

**

I pull into Hangman's driveway and get off my bike. I don't bother knocking, since none of the brothers do when we come here and walk right in. "Melissa?"

"Slammer? Hi, um, what are you doing here?" she asks, walking towards me from the living room. Fucking hell, she's beautiful. Not a stitch of make up and wearing baggy sweats, but she's still the most stunning woman I've ever seen.

"How you feel about goin' on a date with me tomorrow night?"

Her eyes widen as I step closer to her, pulling her body against mine. *Fuck,* I want to take her right here and now. Her body molds to mine like a perfect fit. Feeling her soft body touching mine, too damn good to be true. I've never wanted a woman more than I do her right now.

"Um, does dad know about this?" She pulls back slightly, but I don't loosen my grip on her. I like having her in my arms too much.

I grin, tempted to kiss her already. "Yup, asked him before I came here."

She lets out a small breath. "Wow, um, okay?"

I give her a grin, and she blushes. "Good, I'll be here at six tomorrow night. Wear something sexy." I pinch her on the ass and her face reddens. Not in an embarrassed way but in an *"oh shit, I like this"* way.

"Okay." She breathes out as I lean down into her face.

"Fuck, you're beautiful." She licks her bottom lip, and I can't help it. I crash my lips down on hers, needing to taste her. She doesn't hold back, as her tongue touches mine. She moans, and her hands tangle in my hair as she pulls slightly. My dick is begging to be let out, I don't want to do that right now. I want her to be sure before I shove my cock into her, so I pull back. I know that once I got my cock in her, I'll be ruined, and she'll be mine no matter what.

Her eyes are closed, and she looks dazed. I give her a quick kiss on the nose, let go of her and give her a wink once she opens her eyes. "There'll be more of that tomorrow night, a lot more of that."

I walk out of the house feeling as if I just won the fuckin' lottery. I just got my girl.

Licking my lips as I start my bike, I can still taste her.

So fucking perfect.

So fucking mine.

Chapter 17

Melissa

It's been months since I've last seen Dray. I still miss him, but I know I need to get over it. He's not mine, never has been considering he's married. I've spoken to Trevor and Cori almost every day, well until last weekend when Cori told me to talk to Dray and hear him out. I hung up on her and refused to answer her calls since. It's been hard not to answer her, since I know that she'll be having her baby soon. But I just can't talk to her right now.

How could she want me to talk to that asshole? She knows what he did. *Hell*, a rule we always had was that we would never knowingly sleep with married men, and with Dray being married, well, that makes it twice I've done it. Cori and I slept with brothers once, they were our usual fuck buddies when we didn't want to waste time with one-night stands. When we found out they were married we ended that arrangement instantly. Can't stand cheating bastards.

Trevor understands why I'm staying, especially when I told him about the building dad bought me to turn into a restaurant. He's not a fan of his brother, but he loves that he's treating me so well, and said I'm exactly where I should be. He misses me, all the Angels do, but they understand why I'm staying, too.

"Hey, your sister has been blowing up my phone," Dad tells me as I come out of my room.

I shrug and check on Mikayla. "I don't want to talk to her right now."

"All right. You still sure about tonight?" he asks, sounding different than his usual hard self.

"Yes, I am. Anara said she'll watch Mikayla." Anara is the woman that Dirty wants, but she won't give him the time of day, I don't blame her. We've talked a lot since I met her, and she wants that fairy tale kind of love. She knows with Dirty, he'll never be faithful, so she doesn't even want to chance it. I think she's wrong, though. Yeah, I know most of the men in the Untamed aren't faithful to their women, but Dirty seems different. He seems as if he has a heart and would hate to hurt the woman he loves.

"Let me know if Slammer needs a beat down, you know I would love to dole out that punishment," he says, grinning scarily.

At first, I was gonna say no to Slammer, thinking he was joking, but when I saw he was serious, I said yes. Anyone that can go to my dad and ask for permission to date me, well that's saying something. And the kiss he gave me after I said yes, I'll never forget it. I've never been kissed like that in my life, not even by Dray. I swear it was the best kiss ever. It was full of such passion and longing. I didn't want it to end.

After he left, I started to second guess the date. Would it be too soon to move on? It's been months, but I don't know. After that kiss, I don't know anything anymore. I'm just scared I'm gonna get hurt again, and I not sure if I could handle it, especially with Mikayla. We're a package deal. Her father already hurt her, I don't want another man doing it too, even if she's too young to understand it yet. But then again, I haven't had sex in months, and that kiss left me hornier than I've ever been. If Slammer hadn't left when he did, I would have jumped him. But tonight, if Slammer keeps his promise of more of those kisses, I'm totally getting laid.

There is no reason I shouldn't have fun and try to move on with my life. Sure, I still think about what Dray and I could have had, but then I remember he's a lying sack of shit. I have to think about doing what is right for me and my daughter, and right now, that is staying here and going on this date tonight.

"All right, well, while you were in the shower, I put condoms in your top drawer by your bed. Be safe, and for fuck sake, please don't be too loud. I do not want the cameras I have in the hallway pickin' up sex noises from my own damn kid. I'll be back after your fuckfest."

Even though I'm embarrassed at the thought of the cameras picking up any sex noises, I giggle, reaching out to squeeze his arm, I lean in and kiss his cheek. "Love you, Daddy." Sure, he's a bad man, but Tori was right when she said he was a good father. He's made me feel safe, just as safe as I felt when I grew up living with the Angels.

"Love you too, kid," he says gruffly and stomps to his room, shutting his door.

**

Slammer arrives right on time and surprises me even more because he didn't come on his bike, he's in a newish looking truck.

I open the door as he bounds up the front steps and he grins at me. "Didn't think you could get more beautiful, but you proved me wrong."

I feel myself blush, and I smile at him. "Well, where are we going?"

"Figured we could go to the Ale House, that work for you?"

"Never been, always up for trying new things."

He grins. "Good to know."

As we drive to the restaurant, he tells me his real name is Caden and that apart from the club, he makes custom furniture.

When we get to the restaurant, we talk more about our lives, me telling him everything about my life up until now, him telling me about his.

"Gotta tell you though, being honest here, I've never in my life had a serious relationship before. Booty calls, fuck buddies, one-night stands, but never an actual relationship."

I bite my lip, unsure of what to say.

"But you'll never have to worry about me stepping out on you, ever. I want you, I've made no secret of that, so you gotta know I won't ever hurt you in that way. I'm sure I'll fuck up sometimes, I'm a man, it's what we do, but never in that way. Get me?"

"Um, yeah, I get you."

"Good." In this moment I can't help but fall for him. He sure has a way with words.

"So, where do you live?"

"Don't got a place of my own right now, just living at the club house, but this goes the way I intend for it to go, I'll be buying a place, and soon."

I blush, holy shit, he *really likes* me.

"How many kids you want?" he asks suddenly.

"Uh, I don't know, two or three more, maybe? Why do you wanna know?"

"Need to know how many bedrooms to look for when I buy a house."

My eyes widen. Holy shit, my panties are soaked, and I'm trying my hardest to sit still in my chair, but he senses my movement and his eyes go hungry.

Wanting to move on from this line of talk, we start talking about Mikayla as we finish our meal.

At the end of the night, I really don't want it to end. "Do you want to come in?"

"You invite me in tonight, you do know I'm not leaving until morning, right?"

I feel my panties getting wet, again, and I bite my lip, nodding.

The second I open the front door, Caden slams me against the wall, his lips inches from mine. "You sure this isn't how you got your name," I tease.

He cocks a sexy grin at me before teasing the seam of my lips with his eager tongue. Pulling back slightly he looks at me, "If that's what you want, then you can make it known that's how I got it from now on." He bites my bottom lip gently, before kissing me again.

"Mhmm," I moan, knowing that this kiss is only the beginning.

"You drive me crazy. Have me so damn hard for you."

He takes my hand and puts it over his crotch. Oh my, he feels ... big.

Excitement shoots down to my toes as he kisses me again, sucking my bottom lip into his mouth tenderly. My fingers move up the back of his neck and into his hair.

His hand moves over the waistband of my jeans and undoes the button.

Sliding his fingers into my panties he growls, before rubbing in a circular motion over my clit.

He pulls back, taking his hand with him. I watch with wide eyes as he licks his fingers, "I needed to see how sweet your pussy tasted," He tells me, his voice gravelly.

To my own surprise, I tell him, "Don't stop at just a taste."

"You just may be the death of me. Why don't we continue this in your room?" I nod eagerly as I remember what Dad said about the cameras, and I absolutely do not want my dad to see me getting slammed by Slammer. It's been a while since I have felt so wanted and desired after Dray hurt me so bad.

Caden is sexy and rough but he has a sweet side. Grabbing my hand, he leads me down the hall toward my room.

The moment the door closes behind me, we are on one another ripping our clothes off and falling onto the bed.

He palms my tit before sucking a nipple into his mouth as he lines his cock up with me.

In one smooth thrust Caden is in me, taking his time, moving at a languid pace.

"Fuck, your pussy feels so damn good," his husky voice grits in my ear as he draws out and pushes back in, repeating the motion as he looks into my eyes.

Scratching my nails down his back, I urge him to go faster and harder.

Taking the hint, he brings my knee up over his shoulder, taking me deeper with every slam of his body against mine. His eyes stay on mine the whole time, never breaking our connection. It's intense to say the least.

Bucking my hips, I match his every move, so close to free falling over the edge of orgasmic bliss.

The sex is hot, fast, and dirty … but we both knew it would be. It's exactly what I wanted, what I needed to get me over my dry spell after Dray.

Once we've both gotten off, he leaves me basking in post-orgasmic bliss to go clean up in the bathroom. I smile at him breathlessly as he returns with a washcloth to clean me.

"Rest up and hydrate. We're just getting started." He winks handing me a bottle of water.

A delicious ache for Caden pools between my thighs as he crawls between them, looking at my pussy with eager eyes and a greedy tongue.

Chapter 18

Dray

A month later

My life is in fucking hell, five months since I last saw Melissa and Mikayla, five months since I last even talked to them, and it's fucking killing me. Melissa has me blocked from being able to call, even has me blocked on Facebook, at least the Angels have the decency to forward any pictures that Melissa sends them of Mikayla to me. I had to get shit done before I could make the move to go for her, waiting for the court shit to get over with, finish up my current open cases, and finalizing that bullshit divorce. Thankfully, I'm done, and I can finally do what I need to do. Yesterday morning, I got word that I have the job in Saint John if I can get there in two weeks.

As I finish packing my suitcases my phone starts going off. Now that I think about it, it's been going off constantly for hours, I've just been too busy trying to get on the road to even pay attention to it.

"Yeah?" I answer without looking at the caller ID.

"How could you do this, you bastard?" Shayla screeches.

"For fuck sake." I sigh. "What do you want? Speak quick before I hang up."

"You had me arrested, my kids taken away and given to Layla. You even sold the house?"

"Damn right I did, bitch. Have fun in prison, don't contact me again." I hang up and toss the phone on the bed. I made sure that the money from the sale of the house was all given to Layla to help her out. Not that she needed the money, she's rich, but it's for Laura and Luca. She told me she would put it into a college account for them, and with the amount of money I got from the house and everything in it, minus the kid's stuff, they could both go onto be doctors or some other expensive career choice.

Over the last few weeks, I've been in touch with the kids often. They still struggle with not calling me dad, and I get it, being called Uncle Dray feels wrong to me too. I promised them the minute I got back from getting my woman and kid, I will plan for them to come over for a weekend and spend it with us.

My phone goes off again as I zip my last suitcase, and I see it's Cori calling me. *Shit,* probably wants to bitch me out again.

"Hey, Cori," I answer politely.

She sniffs. "I'm sorry I didn't let you talk the last time we spoke. I acted like a bitch." The Angels must have told her my story.

"Nothing to apologize for, girl, you were right in your anger. I should have told Melissa about my ex."

"This is true, but at the same time we shouldn't have all jumped to conclusions." This is a side of Cori I've never seen before, getting knocked up changed her completely. In a good way.

"I'm packing up now to go get your sister, any advice for me?"

Cori giggles. "Just be you, Dray, she'll fight you. In case you haven't noticed, she's more stubborn than I am. But eventually, she'll hear you out."

"Thanks." I smile into the phone.

"I'll let you go, text me, keep me updated?"

"Promise. Tell Blake I said hi."

"Just bring my sister and my niece home. I miss them."

"Me too," I tell her softly.

I've been without my should be wife and daughter for far too long.

We hang up and I lug my shit down to my truck. The drive should take me five days with stops, but I'm gonna try my hardest to only stop when I need to, so I can get there faster. I need her back. At the very least, I need my kid. I miss her.

Flashback Chapter

Dray

Enough is enough

Two fucking months since I fucked it all up with Melissa. I was drunk as hell the night I had her, knocked her up, and didn't even know it. I can't remember a damn thing about that night. We knew someone was slipping drugs at the Club, hence my post here, and I was the dumb fuck that had enough of watching Melissa fuck around with other guys and had a few drinks. Next thing I knew I was waking up in some chick's apartment and couldn't remember a fucking thing that happened. Only thing I recall is being livid about seeing Melissa.

It wasn't until last month when Blake came pounding at my door calling me every name in the book saying I knocked Melissa up. I'm such an idiot. Every day since then, I've forced my way into Melissa's life, and so far, she keeps pushing back against it. I've wanted her since I first saw her, and it was a kick to the fucking gut to find out she was underage.

She was right when she said Randy didn't care she was in the club, but the second he told me she wasn't legal, I had enough of watching her ass strut around me, so I kicked her out.

Cori and Blake keep telling me to keep trying, and they must think I'm fucking stupid if they think I'll do otherwise. She's carrying my kid. She's mine. And if Melissa thinks she can keep trying to push me away she's got another thing coming. Not gonna happen.

I bound up the stairs to Melissa and Cori's condo and pound on the door. Today is the day, this shit ends. It doesn't take long before the door is open, and Melissa is standing there, glaring at me.

"What do you want now?" she snaps at me.

I shove her slightly back, so I can come in and shut her door. "This is done," I state.

Her eyes widen.

"You and I are gonna clear our shit up, and then we're moving on. Together. You and me, and our child. I don't remember a thing that happened the night I finally had you. I wanted you since you were jailbait but couldn't act on it. I was

drunk as fuck that night, and I can't apologize enough for what happened." I don't tell her I was actually drugged, because then I'd have to reveal more shit to her, and I can't. "I want you, only you. I want this child we've created. And as soon as you can make it happen, I want to marry you. I never believed in that love at first sight shit, but I knew it with you."

Her breathing is labored. "I'm sick of seeing you with other men, I'm sick of not having you as mine. Fuck. Melissa. I fucking love you."

She closes her eyes and turns away from me. "I was only with those other guys because I wanted you, but you didn't seem to care."

I move in close, making her look at me. "Trust me, I care, too fucking much. I love you."

"I love you too," she whispers. There, done, this seals it. I kiss her, and this time, when I make love to her, I'm gonna remember every fucking moment of it.

Chapter 19

Melissa

After my night with Caden, I've seen him every day, and once a week Anara babysits for me, so we can go out for a date night. It's perfect, almost too perfect. I tried not to fall for Caden, but he's making it impossible, the way he is with Mikayla, how he treats me, the way he fucks me and the way he makes love to me. It's everything I've ever wished for. He's quickly becoming a permanent fixture in our everyday lives. I can see my daughter getting attached too.

Today he picked me up and dropped me off at a salon to get my hair and nails done. He said he wants to pamper me. That, because I am a single mom, he is sure I don't take time out for myself and he wants to give that to me. *So freaking sweet*. I've never had a guy treat me like this before. Not even Dray was this sweet to me. It's refreshing and unexpected coming from a badass outlaw.

Next stop after getting my hair done is a new dress and matching shoes.

I bought his favorite color, blue, along with some sexy matching undergarments.

Caden makes me feel sexy ... *wanted.*

I smile all the time thanks to him.

I leave the shops feeling like I won the lottery and smile the whole way home.

As usual, Caden is right on time, and when I open the door to greet him, my breath rushes out. Holy hell, he's hot. For once he's not wearing his cut, a tee shirt and jeans. Well, the jeans are still there, but they're nice jeans, not a stain or a hole to be found. He has a nice black button-down shirt on, and his hair is pulled back neatly.

"Ready to go?" he asks, his voice gruff, as if he's fighting the urge to shove me against the wall, so he can have his way with me. I have to say that sounds like a damn good idea right now.

I smile and push him back slightly, so I can get out the door and lock it. "Where are we going?" I ask as he leads me to the passenger side, opening the door for me.

When he gets in on his side, he finally tells me where we're going. "Since we're dressed up nice, I figured we could go to Italian by Night. It's a newer place in town, best pasta I've ever eaten honestly."

When we get to the restaurant, I notice a line that's half way down the street. "Um, Caden, it looks like we could be waiting a long ass time."

"Don't worry about it. I made reservations. This place is hit or miss with walk ins, maybe three of those groups will get in tonight, but the rest for sure won't."

"Mr. Brennan, your table is ready. Follow me," the hostess says as soon as we bypass everyone waiting in line. That's odd, he didn't even go up to her to give him his name. Maybe he just comes here a lot?

Once we're seated and left to look over the menus, Caden puts his hand over mine. "Let me tonight?"

I raise my brows. "Okay, fine, just nothing with seafood remember, gag." He laughs at my face and winks. Dad brought home some fish and lobster once, and Caden and a few other members of the club came over for a cookout. I'd never had fish or lobster before, although fish sticks don't technically count. As I tried to take a bite, the smell alone smelled like a rotting vagina and the taste ... I will never forget it. So awful. Now anytime someone brings up eating seafood, I gag.

"So how did the hostess know you when you didn't even check in yet?"

"Could be the fact that I was the reason this place looks as beautiful as it does," he informs me as he throws his arms out wide.

"Oh, you mean you designed and built all this?" I ask, nodding to the tables and chairs the booths and even the bar area.

"Yeah, instead of payment for all the work I did, I requested twenty five percent of the business. Works out well, not only that I also own this building, so with getting my percent of the profits, I get twelve grand a month off this place in rent alone."

Wow. "That's amazing. Would you be willing to work on my restaurant too?"

"Already was planning on it." He shoots me a wink and I smile.

The waitress comes over, and Caden places our orders so fast I have no clue what he said. All I know is, he said a lot of things. "You trying to fatten me up?" I ask when the waitress walks away.

He chuckles and reaches for my hands across the table. "I enjoy spending time with you."

I blush and give his hands a little squeeze. "I more than enjoy spending time with you, you're far better than any man I could ever have dreamed up. Your amazing with my daughter, you treat me with so much kindness and respect. Honestly, it's a little scary, with how I'm feeling, all this emotion and love is just overwhelming."

His eyes flare with lust. "I was gonna tell you to savor the food, but I'm thinking once it's out, eat fast. I need to get you home and out of those clothes."

Chapter 20

Slammer

We eat as quickly as we can without making ourselves get sick and rush home. I notice as I pull into the driveway that Hangman ain't here. Good. Because I'm gonna be making his daughter scream my name a million times tonight, and the old bastard doesn't need to hear it.

I jog around to her side and pull her out as she giggles. "Someone is in a hurry."

"Yeah, to get inside, but once we're in there, we won't be in any hurry." I'm taking my fuckin' time. "Hope you're not tired."

I grab her keys from her and unlock the door, quickly pulling her in with me and slam the door shut. I shove her into the door, while locking it, and crush my mouth down on hers.

I walk Melissa into her bedroom while we rip each other's clothes off along the way. I can't wait to get her naked.

Closing the door behind us, I order, "Up on the bed and on your back." I slowly make my way to her. Smirking at her as she licks her lips.

Heading into bed, I place my face into her warm pussy. The smell is intoxicating. Licking, sucking, finger-fucking, her fucking response has me over the edge. I work her pussy over as she clenches her muscles tight. Humming on her clit, I move my fingers inside her in a come-here motion, hitting her sweet spot. Her warmth coats my fingers and her knees shake.

My girl is so close to getting off.

I increase the tempo and suck her sweet nub harder, nipping at her with my teeth.

Her hands find my hair and pull as she screams out she's coming.

"Fuck, yeah," I murmur.

I lick up all her juices as she keeps grinding into my face, I don't want to stop mouth-fucking her, but my dick needs love too.

"Get up, let me lay down so you can sit on my face."

Her eyes bug out. "But you just made me cum that way already."

"Yeah, and I ain't fucking done, you're gonna suck my cock while I eat you out this time."

She bites her bottom lip and moans as she moves onto my face. Looking at her pussy dripping wet, fuck. "Fuckin' love this cunt," I say as I quickly give her a lick. As she starts grinding on my face, she finally starts sucking my cock and stroking my balls. *Fuck yes,* this is so damn good. I pull away from her cunt and growl, "I'm gonna cum soon baby, you just keep sucking until I make you cum again, you don't stop." She moans against my cock and I go back to working her beautiful pussy.

She changes her movements, sucking me as if she's a god damned vacuum, while using her hand to help pump my cock. It doesn't take long for me to explode in her mouth, and she does exactly what I told her to do, she doesn't let up, she swallows my load like a fuckin' pornstar.

I stop tongue fucking her and move to her clit, wrapping my lips around it and suck, as she slowly keeps at my dick, cleaning every last bit of cum off it. The way her mouth feels, there is no way in fuck my cock will stop being hard. Finally, after a few more minutes of me sucking her clit, she comes, and I move my tongue, shoving it inside her, tasting her. I groan in ecstasy.

She collapses on top of me, panting as if she just ran a marathon. "I swear your cock just got bigger," she says in awe.

I chuckle. "Baby, that's because your face is still right there and your cunt juice is all over my face."

"You're insatiable." She giggles as I toss her legs off me, but not before giving her pussy one last kiss that has her moaning.

"I ain't done with you yet." I flip her onto her stomach, shoving my hand underneath her to cup her pussy, pushing a finger inside her still drenched cunt. "Ass up, baby, as much as my cock loved your mouth, he really needs your pussy now."

Hours later, it seems as if we've finally had enough of each other, for now. "Fuck, you taste good when you come," I tell her as she climbs off me after swallowing my load, for the third time tonight.

"Same to you, big guy." She gives me a wink and licks her way up my chest, straddling my still hard cock.

As she sinks down on me, I grab her hips, and sit up, sucking a nipple into my mouth. *"Fuck yes."* Goddamn she is so tight and fits to my dick perfectly.

Letting her hips go, my hands go to her ass. "Who's insatiable now, baby?"

"Just shut up and fuck me," she breathes.

"My pleasure," I reply as I lift her ass up and slam her back down on me.

Chapter 21

Dray

Pounding on the front door of Hangman's house I wait and wait. Finally, it opens. I don't give a shit that it's two in the morning and that there seems to be company over, I've driven for four days to get here as fast as I could, and I'm not leaving without her.

"You," Hangman snarls at me.

"Where is she?"

He crosses his arms and stares at me. It's a scare tactic, I know, but I'm not leaving.

"She doesn't want to see you."

"Well too bad, she's going to see me, and she's going to damn well listen," I shout at him.

"Dad? What's going on?" I hear Melissa's sleepy voice ask.

"An unwanted visitor."

I stare at him, hoping he'll see the desperation in my eyes to let me in. He takes a step back to let me inside. But before I fully make it in, he wraps a hand around my throat and gets in my face. "You fuck her up anymore than she already is, I don't care what she says, your body will never be found."

I gulp, and he moves away. I know he doesn't make empty threats. If he wants me dead, I'll be dead.

"Hangman, you can stay for this chat. I want to make sure Melissa doesn't jump to conclusions, you can help me keep her shut up until I'm done."

"Slammer still in bed?" Hangman asks her, without replying to me.

I see Melissa give him a small nod and looks at him with wide eyes. This has me stiffening. Who the fuck is Slammer and how would Melissa know he's still in bed?

I don't let this bother me right now, because I need to talk to her. Explain.

I drag Melissa along behind me as I follow Hangman into his living room. I sit her down, and Hangman stands behind the couch, arms folded.

"You have to listen to me. Okay. Promise?"

Her jaw clenches and she nods—finally.

"I was eighteen when I got married to Shayla. She found out she was pregnant, she said it was mine, and I had no reason to doubt her, ever. I wanted to do right by her, so we got married. Three years later, she was pregnant again. I was

119

happy. Over the moon happy. Until I came home from work early one day and found her and my brother together." Melissa gasps. "I forgave her for it. But when Laura was eight years old, she got sick, and when the tests came back saying I wasn't a match, I got a DNA test. Both those kids weren't mine." I leave out how I almost beat Matt to death.

"Oh Drayton," Melissa whispers, grabbing my hand. "What was she sick from?"

I shrug, "One of her kidneys was failing, doctors don't know how it happened, since she was so young. I know you really only need one to live, but she was a kid, still is, so I made sure she got a replacement. Unfortunately, it wasn't me. I thought for sure it would be, I don't need two you know. When the results came back the doctor said I wasn't a match, but I had similar markers and that there was a high chance her father would be an exact match. That fucking threw me, because I was her father. Little did I know; my whole damn marriage was a lie."

She gives my hand a squeeze, and I continue.

"I left, filed for divorce. I could have forgiven the cheating, but to know those kids weren't mine, I couldn't forgive that. I thought I was divorced, I had the paperwork and everything. When Shayla showed up saying we were still married, I thought she was lying. Turns out she and my brother forged the divorce decree that was sent to me." I bring her hand to my face, kissing it. "I never would have started anything with you if I thought for even a second I was still married. You have to believe me."

She's quiet for a few moments before she answers. "Why couldn't you have told me all of this? We've been together for a long time now."

"I wanted to, but every time I started to think of Laura and Luca, the two kids I thought were mine, it would kill me inside. And I know what you're like. You and Cori would have gotten a wild hair and tracked Shayla down."

Melissa snorts. "True," she mutters.

"There's something else, though."

"Spit it out then, boy," Hangman barks, losing patience with the situation. "I'd like to go back to bed at some point tonight."

"Dad? Maybe you could leave the room for a moment? Please?" she asks him, and he nods and stomps off.

"I'm not a bouncer," I tell her when she looks at me.

"What?" Melissa says, looking confused. "Dude, I've been to the club, I know what you are."

I shake my head. "I'm an undercover cop for the Red Deer Police department. Well, as of now, since my cover was blown, I'm just a cop, not even my ex-wife knew. She sort of always had something against cops, so yeah, I even lied to her all the time about what I really did for work." Something I hated doing at the time, but now, I don't regret it at all, considering I was able to put her and my brother down for the crimes they did.

"Get out!" She snaps. "All this time together, and you've never been honest with me. I can't believe you."

"Melly, just listen to me."

"She said to get out. You don't, I'll put you out. You fuck," a man I don't know growls at me, walking into the living room, and his arm wraps around my woman.

"The fuck? Who are you?" I shout at him.

His arm trails around the front of Melissa's stomach, his hand rubbing her, and I have the urge to break the fucker's hand. Who does he think he is, touching the woman who should be my wife like that?

"I'm the man that saw stars all night because of this hot bitch, that's all you need to know. She told you to leave, so fuckin' leave."

Melissa stiffens at his words, and she looks away from me. I stagger back. Did I lose her for good? Did I wait too long to get her back? Knowing I'm not going to get any answers tonight, I hang my head down. "I'll leave tonight, but I'm coming back tomorrow. I want to see my daughter." I start to say more but seeing her with another man fucking cuts deep. Too damn deep, reminding me of the past even if the situation is different this time.

I storm out of the house feeling like shit. I destroyed us. I sent her running, she was standing in another man's arms. Can I win her back? Will she ever forgive me?

Fuck, I hope so.

I need her.

We should be a family.

I get in my vehicle and sit outside the house a while longer, trying to calm down before I drive.

She's moved on, but I won't give up so easily.

Chapter 22

Slammer

I keep Melissa in my arms as the front door slams shut. With Dray here, what does that mean for us? "Are you okay?" I ask.

She shakes her head. "I honestly don't know. I've known him for years, have a child with him, and not once did I really know anything about him."

She turns in my arms and looks up at me and bites her lip. "I'm sorry you had to be here when he finally showed up."

"I'm not, I'll always be here for you, you know that. And I know your head is probably all sorts of fucked up right now, so if you want me to leave to give you some space, I will. I'll do whatever you need me to do." I take a breath and tilt her chin up, so she's looking right at me. "You do need to talk with him, though. He is Mikayla's father."

"I just want you with me. I don't want to think about Dray right now. Since he's apparently not leaving town, there is no reason to stress at this moment." She gives me a small smile.

"There aren't many men like you out there. Thank you for being all that you are." She presses her lips to mine softly, and then steps back.

Fuck, I love her. I want to tell her, but I'm worried that will just muddle her head more. I'll tell her soon, and fuck, I'm happy she doesn't want me to leave right now. It would kill me, but I'd do anything for her.

Anything.

We're meant to be together. I want her. I want a family with her and her daughter.

**

Melissa

All this time together, with Dray, it was all a lie. Was anything he ever told me the truth? I love how Caden was here with me, God only knows how I would have reacted had he not taken a stand by my side when Dray was here.

"Melissa, come on, stop thinking, go back to bed with Slammer. He said he'll be back tomorrow, I have to go out of town for a few days, but I'll make sure Slammer stays here and Dirty comes to keep an eye on shit," Dad says, coming back into the room.

"Come on." Caden tugs my hand, giving dad a chin lift and I follow behind him, down the hall and to my room.

Once the door closes I take in all that is Caden, my handsome, sweet, loving, biker. My feelings are all messed up, I love Dray, have for a while, but staring at Caden, I feel as if my heart has been ripped into two, and I move, shoving Caden onto my bed and climbing on top of him.

His hands come up on my ass and they squeeze as I lean down to kiss him. "I know you won't like what I'm about to say, but I'm going to say it anyways." His brows furrow and he nods, still holding me tight. "I love Dray, have for a long time." His body stills under me, his face shutting down. "But, the last month of being with you, learning all there is to learn about you, how you treat my daughter, how you treat me, I've found myself falling in love with you too." At that his body completely relaxes and he crushes me down to him.

"Fuck, Melissa, I love you too." My head comes up and tears swim in my eyes. "I know this isn't easy for you, but I swear, fuckin' vow to you, I'll do anything I can to make you happy."

He moves fast, flipping me over to my back and tugging my robe off me in a frenzy, I moan when his lips wrap around my nipple as one of his hands moves down, cupping my pussy. "I need you in me," I breathe out, feeling as if I will burst without him inside me.

"*Fuck.*" He grunts, surging up, sliding inside me hard and fast.

Caden's body presses down on mine as our hips rub together creating a delicious friction. He's being so fucking sweet, kissing me tenderly and whispering sweet nothings about how he wants to take care of me. How I make him want to be a better man.

As his tongue plunges in my mouth, brushing against mine, I could cry because I am falling so in love with him, but there is still a huge part of my heart that cares for Dray.

How can I love them both?

As Caden pumps into me, I push those thoughts aside and allow him to make love to me. Showing me that he can be gentle, but he can also be rough as he grips my hips, holding me still as he takes what he wants.

"Your pussy was made for me, made to fit perfectly to my dick." His fingers rub over my clit as he moves in and out in a hypnotic rhythm. "Roll over, want you from behind."

I do as he says — face down, ass up. With one hand tangled in my hair and the other lining him up with my slick heat, he rams into me with raw, dominating force. Yanking my head back, he growls in my ear. "My dirty girl likes it hard. Don't you?" Slammer slams into me hard. I still say this is exactly how he got his name.

"Yes," I pant out in a barely there whisper.

"Can't hear you." He tugs my head back harder, not in pain but wicked pleasure.

Chapter 23

Dray

I barely slept last night, seeing Melissa in another man's arm killed me. She might be with someone else right now, but I also saw the way she looked at me too. She still loves me. I know she does, and considering we have a child together, that must count for something. I just need to figure out what the hell I'm going to do. Need to find out everything I can about the fucker that's touching my woman.

I get to the police station and my desk is already covered in paperwork. Doesn't look like I'll be starting my first day off light. I get to work reading everything I need to, so I can do my job properly. Four hours later, I know all about the Untamed MC and the local rival club, the Jacks Devils. Both clubs are seriously fucked up, but so far, nothing that can get any members locked up for good, or anything that will stick.

I flip back through the file on the Untamed and stumble across the picture of the man that was with Melissa last night. Caden 'Slammer' Brennan, twenty-eight years old, and other than a few stints in prison for violence, seems he has a habit of losing his temper easily, there isn't anything else there about him. This is the man Melissa has around my daughter?

Fuck, it's bad enough her father is around her, but that's different. This man has no right to be around.

I get a text and see it's from Melissa.

We'll be at the park on Champlain Drive in about an hour. If you want to see Mikayla, meet us there. – Melissa.

I check the time and agree to the meet. *Fuck*, I miss my kid. Hopefully Melissa leaves the biker at home, so I can convince her to come back to me. She may think I did her wrong, and in ways I did by not being upfront, but I love her. I just have to show her … prove to her, she's mine. She has always been *mine*.

**

Melissa

"I can't believe she wanted to share her ice cream with you," I tease Caden.

Giving me a sly grin, he winks and says, "I have that effect on women."

"Is that so?"

"Yup." He leans in and quickly pecks my lips, smearing chocolate fudge over my lips where my baby girl has been feeding him the rest of her treat.

"Ass," I whisper as he hands me a napkin. There is something seriously fucking hot about seeing this tattooed tough guy at my daughter's mercy though. Whatever she wants he gives it to her within reason. More ice cream ended up on his face than in his mouth, but he didn't get annoyed at all, he just laughed.

"You should probably get that cleaned up."

I watch in awe as he wipes down Mikayla's tiny hands with wipes and checks the front of her shirt, telling her, "Want you to be all clean when you see your dad."

My heart melts. I am sure this is difficult for him, being here with us to meet Dray. I want to say something to him but don't get the chance. He is so gentle with her. Before we even left to come, he was double checking to make sure we had everything she could possibly need in her bag, just as a dad would. As Dray should be doing. I know I took that away from him by moving so far away, but I didn't think he'd come here. I didn't think he would even care considering what I thought to be true about him.

We're at the park not even ten minutes when a police cruiser pulls into the lot and out comes Dray.

He glares at me when he notices Caden is here. *Shit*, maybe I should have mentioned that when I texted him. Caden told me he would send someone to watch for me, but instead I asked if he could come himself.

I probably should have kept my mouth shut. It's just that I love being with him. Not to mention I am nervous about seeing Dray again. I probably should have brought Anara, but I wasn't thinking.

"Melissa, what's he doing here?" Dray demands angrily.

"He's here with me, Dray, you're here to spend time with your daughter."

I watch Mikayla dump sand down her shirt and smile.

"Why don't you leave, let me have time with my family," he snarls at Caden.

"Your daughter is right there, why don't you back out of my face, and spend time with her. You got a problem with me? Take it up with me when the kid ain't around. She doesn't need to see her father being a jackass," Caden snaps back at him, quietly so Mikayla doesn't hear.

Right now, Dray is making himself look like an ass, and it's making me second guess everything about him. I feel like I never really knew the man I made a child with.

Chapter 24

Slammer

Dray finally stalks off and bends down to Mikayla, who finally notices him. She lets out a loud screech, "Daddy!"

My heart twists at hearing her say that, I know it shouldn't, she's not my daughter, but *fuck,* I wish she was.

"Thank you for being so good about him getting in your face," Melissa says quietly to me as we sit on the picnic tables away from Dray and Mikayla.

"He might not like me, and I get it. I don't like him either, but I respect him as Mikayla's dad, and she doesn't need to see two grown ass men fighting like idiots."

She smiles, and it makes me want to kiss her, but I don't. I'm trying to be a fucking respectful fuck right now in front of Dray, but it's killing me. Melissa grabs my hand and gives me a squeeze as we continue to watch the father daughter duo play in the sand.

An hour later, Dray carries Mikayla to us and passes her over to Melissa without even looking in my direction.

"I get you're still pissed and don't want to talk with me yet, I get it. But I have next weekend off and I was hoping you'd let me have her for the weekend."

I look to Melissa and her eyes widen. "Yeah, that um, that would be fine. She'd love that."

"Good, thanks." He chews his lip and sighs. "We still need to talk too, and I'm hoping you'll let me do that."

I step in. "We'll work that out, when Melissa wants to talk with you, I'll keep an eye on Mikayla."

Dray's head shoots back, and he looks shocked I would offer that up. He stares at me for a minute and then nods.

"I'll text." With that he walks off.

"That was different," Melissa says.

I agree, but I also feel as if he's got something up his sleeve. I don't have a good feeling.

If he is coming for what I see as mine, I'll be ready. I'm not taking any chances when it comes to my woman or her child.

Chapter 25

Melissa

The last few weeks have been somewhat peaceful. Dray and I still haven't talked, but I know it's coming, and it's coming soon. Caden has even told me I need to chat with him, to co-parent for Mikayla's sake, and I agree on that. But I'm also scared that talking with Dray will have me back with him again, and I don't want to hurt Caden if it comes to that, because I also don't want to give him up.

Dray has Mikayla this weekend and Caden had to do something for the club. So I'm relaxing for once, doing nothing, maybe some reading after I finish putting these dishes away.

A knock on the door has me quickly setting the plate I was drying down and answering the door. I stare in shock. How?

"Stop staring at me, and let me in."

I glance at the time and see that Dad is supposed to be home soon. I pray he's early.

"What are you doing here, mom?"

She pushes past me and goes up the stairs to the living room, pacing. "I got out of jail a month ago and found out Hangman wants me dead or alive." Hearing that doesn't shock me, not anymore. Things I've learned about my dad's club life doesn't even faze me now. "It's been known around that he listens to you, since he didn't hurt your baby daddy. So you need to tell him to back off me. Please."

She grabs my arms so tight, I know I'll have bruising from this. "Why would I save you from him?" She honestly must be nuts to think I'd call off dad from hunting her down.

Her eyes narrow at me. "*I gave birth to you, you shit*!" she yells. She shoves me, and I fall to the floor. "I could have aborted you the second I knew I was pregnant. But no, I kept you. You should be thanking me. But no, you're just as worthless and useless as I thought you were." She sneers.

I get up from the floor, but before I fully stand up, she backhands me across the face.

"You and your sister have been nothing but thorns in my side for years. Fucking ungrateful brats." She grabs my hair, making me stand up. "You're gonna call him off me, or I'll make sure your bastard child never sees you again." She starts cackling. "What's funny is that I was always right. Cori became a gold digger, I don't know what that husband of hers was thinking, tying himself to her forever. And you are worthless. Couldn't even keep your man." She tugs harder on my hair.

Fear grips at me and before she lets go of my hair, the front door crashes open. Mom lets me go instantly and she looks scared. I look up and see my dad, Rage, Dirty, and Caden standing at the opening of the living room, guns drawn.

"You okay, kid?" Dad asks.

"Yeah," I croak out.

"Carson…" Mom starts to say.

"Shut the fuck up, you cunt," he growls. "Where's Mikayla?" he asks me.

"She's at her dad's."

He nods. And walks over to mom and grabs her forcefully. "Melissa, please, call him off! Don't let him kill your mama," she begs.

She doesn't stop screaming so dad shuts her up by punching her in the mouth. Holy shit. My eyes go wide. "You shut the fuck up right now, Luanne. Trust me, you'll need to save the screaming for later." I start shaking, suddenly terrified. Mom shuts up instantly, tears streaming down her face. "Rage, shoot her up. Otherwise you know she'll start screaming like a banshee when we walk out of this house. Slammer, get the cage going."

Caden quickly kisses me. "I'll be back soon", he tells me and heads out the door.

Rage comes forward with a needle filled with something, and a minute after he injects her with it, you can tell she's as high as a kite.

"Get on your phone, kid. Call your sister. Tell her she'll never have to worry about this bitch again." He hands mom off to Dirty and they leave. Dad comes to me and kisses my forehead. "She'll pay," he vows and walks off.

After everything my mother put Corinne and I through, she deserves what's coming to her. The years in foster care with the sick fucks that had Cori raped, the times our mother would show up tear us down and make our lives hell just as we were finally becoming better. All of it's finally over.

Chapter 26

Hangman

We get to the club house quickly and carry this bitch inside. Rage called ahead and had the place emptied out, only members. I throw her on the floor. "The second she comes down from this high, we'll start," I tell the room. It's gonna take a few hours for the heroin to wear off, so we may as well have some fun. "Boys, if you want a piece of her before we start tearing her apart, I suggest getting on it now." I grin at them and watch as a Dirty, Rage, and a few other members surround her and start tearing her clothes off.

I don't need to watch, normally I jack off when the men do this, but this bitch has my dick shriveled up. Can't believe I fucked her. I'm half tempted to cut my dick off because obviously it's fucked up. I grab a bottle of whiskey and go to my office while the men have their fun with the bitch. And sure enough, Slammer follows me, I knew he was good enough for my kid. Soon enough, I'll make Luanne pay for what she did to my daughter and her sister.

**

"Hangman, we're done, and she's alert, trying to escape, I say it's time," Rage tells me, coming into my office.

I nod and get up, following him out of the room. She's been gagged and is pinned down by Dirty and Slammer. I smile and grab one of the knives that hangs on the wall in the room. She starts shaking her head and tries to move away from the men holding her. Seeing her fear has me grinning bigger. I love this. I walk over to her and make quick work of slicing off her left nipple, she screams, but it's muffled due to the gag. Instantly I rip the tape off her mouth grabbing a chair and sit in front of her.

"You kept my daughter from me. You hurt her, her sister, the things they went through because of you, were vile. You will be getting tortured by me until your last breath, and bitch, I'll smile the whole time."

"Please, don't do this. I'll leave, I won't say anything, I'll never contact the girls again. Just let me go."

"Oh, I'll let you go, after you take your last breath." With those words she screams, and I carry on, taking my time.

Hours later she's passed out from the pain, but not yet dead. I'm surprised the bitch lasted this long.

"Grab me the rope, throw it around that beam." I tell the men, pointing to the beam in the room. Making quick work of what I asked I grab one end, tying it tight around her neck.

"Hoist her up the moment she comes back to, then have her hung until she's dead. I'm gonna get cleaned up now, then head home, Slammer let me have tonight with Melissa."

His jaw clenches, but he nods and heads towards the back of the clubhouse, where his room is.

I take one last look at Luanne, and since learning of my brother not being dead, and of my daughter I never knew, I finally feel peace.

Chapter 27

Melissa

It took me a few minutes to move from my spot once everyone left with my mother. Instantly, I ran to find my phone and hit call on Cori's name.

"'Lo?" she answers sleepily.

"Hey sis, um, sorry for calling so late, but Dad said I needed to."

Instantly, her voice loses the sleepy sound and she sounds alert, more alert than I do right now. "What's going on? Is everything okay?"

"Cori? What's going on?" I hear Blake's concerned voice ask.

"Well, Mom showed up here," I tell her.

"What!?" she screeches. "How did she even know where you were? How did she find you?"

"I don't know, I'm so confused right now, but I don't think she'll be bothering us again. Ever."

"Tell me everything, and Blake, shut the fuck up, I'm on the phone here." I hear Blake grumble in the background and try not to laugh.

"She showed up, was her normal crazy-assed self, and then Dad and the club were here, taking her away." I leave out the drugging her up stuff and of course hitting her.

"Well, at least we know now we really won't ever hear from her again. Does it make me a bad person to say I'm not sorry in the least that your dad probably gutted that bitch for us?"

"If it makes you a bad person, it makes me one also, because honestly, as much as I'm freaked out right now, I feel peace," I whisper.

"Oh Melly," she whispers back.

We end up talking for a little while longer, not about Mom stuff, but just life in general, especially since we've been so out of touch with each other lately. She doesn't really say much when I speak about Caden and Dray, she just listens, which is surprising, since she has a big mouth and an opinion about everything. Just having her listen feels great.

I end up having to let her go as her breathing changes, and she mutters, "Oh shit, gotta go, sis. Looks like this baby is coming." She hangs up quickly with the promise of calling me later. I stay sitting on the couch, waiting for Dad. I want to know everything, I want to know how he knew she was here.

It's just after two in the morning when he comes in and he walks right to me, taking me in his arms and hugging me tightly.

"How did you know she was here?"

"The house is bugged. Cameras everywhere. With my life, I had to have this shit in here. Never know who is gonna come after me. Watching her walk into this house, put her hands on you, say the shit she said, had my blood boiling." I tear up, holding onto him tightly, my face smooshed into his cut.

"What happened to her?"

"Club business, you don't need to know. All you need to know is that she'll never bother you or your sister again."

I sniffle into his chest, I'm sure his shirt will be covered in snot.

"You're not worthless, useless. Nothing she said is true," he assures me. It's like he knew what I was thinking.

**

I awaken in the morning to Caden's beard tickling my thighs. "Hey," I say with a slight yawn. "Whatcha doing?"

"Came over for breakfast." He grins at me with lust-filled eyes.

Heat blooms on my cheeks. "What about Mikayla?" I ask, knowing that Dray is supposed to be dropping her off this morning.

"I locked the door and your dad said if she shows up while we're busy he'll take her out to play for a bit." He pushes the shirt I slept in up over my stomach. His touch sears my skin as he kisses a path to my navel. "Can't stop thinking about you," he whispers.

I moan as he nips at me.

"I wanted to come last night, but Hangman said he wanted to have time with you, just about killed me that I couldn't be here."

"Shh, less talking, more fucking."

Caden chuckles. "As you wish."

Chapter 28

Slammer

Having Melissa is everything I never knew I wanted, shitty part is, I'm starting to have a heart. Dray is still around and doesn't look like he's going anywhere. Can't fault the fucker, I wouldn't want to be away from my kid either. I just wish he didn't still think he had a shot with the woman I love.

I know Melissa still loves him, and it kills me. But I can't fault her for it. He's the father of the beautiful little girl they created. What I have to do next will gut me.

"Can we talk?" I ask her, walking into the kitchen, watching her putting some cereal on Mikayla's highchair.

She frowns. "Everything okay?"

"When you meet up with Dray, I think you should hear him out. Really truly hear him out," I say, refusing to meet her eyes.

I hear her gasp and can't help but stare at her. "You're breaking up with me?"

I grab her roughly, pulling her into me. "Fuck no, I'm not breaking up with you. This kills me, but you need to hear the guy out. As much as this kills me, I know you still have feelings for him, and I'm willing to step aside if he's who you want."

Her body starts to shake against me, and I feel her tears wet my shirt.

"I don't want to be without you, though," she whispers.

"Then don't, but the choice needs to be yours. Even if it means I step aside, or you are with both of us."

She pushes me back slightly. Looking confused. "Both of you? Like a threesome? Cheating scenario? I don't get it."

I chuckle slightly, cupping her face. "Nothing like that, no threesomes, no cheating. I meant, until you can figure out who you want, who you truly can't be without, date both of us."

She gulps and shakes her head slightly. "Dray would never go for that."

"Then he loses out automatically. I hate this, fuckin' hate it beyond anything, but if it means keeping you a while longer, then I'm willing to do anything to make sure that happens."

"Why are you doing this, Caden?"

"Like I said, I love you and will do anything to see you happy."

She shakes her head. "I don't deserve you."

"It's me that doesn't deserve you." I tell her, kissing her softly. My phone starts going off in my pocket as I start to kiss her deeper. "Shit, that's the club, I should be back tonight, if you can get a hold of Dray and he agrees to meet up with you, let me know. I'll come and stay with Mikayla."

She gives me a small smile as I give her a quick kiss and head out.

Chapter 29

Dray

Hauling my ass into work for the early shift, I dread what's awaiting me at my desk. Most likely more shit about the Jacks Devils. I keep getting files about them, but so far not one ounce of proof so we can get the bastards off the streets.

Three hours later, it's finally break time. As I get up to grab some coffee my phone pings with a text. Looking at it, I see it's from Melissa.

Can we talk? Tonight? - M

I don't even hesitate in replying as hope flares in my chest. I'm hoping this is a good talk, one that will have us back together, the way we belong.

Yes, 7 work? - D

Ok, just the two of us, Mikayla will stay home with Caden. - M

As much as I don't want that fucker near Melissa or Mikayla, I'll allow this. I wonder if he knows she's meeting up with me tonight. Thinking on it, I shoot her another text.

Want me to pick up you? – D

That works, see you later – M

I frown, part of me was thinking she would say no and want to meet up somewhere, which had me hoping she was maybe doing this behind Slammer's back. Instead the dick is babysitting my kid, while I pick Melissa up.

Now I'm thinking it's possible that this talk might not be what I'm thinking. I can't let her be done with me, I just can't.

**

I pull into Hangman's driveway and notice the lights on in the house. Before I even get the chance to turn off the engine, the front door opens and Melissa steps out, with Slammer slightly behind her. Fuck, she's beautiful, her hair blows in the wind, and she's wearing ripped jeans that look amazing on her. I bought her those jeans just after she had our daughter, I still remember how perfect her ass looks in them. She zips up her blue Old Navy hoodie, looks at me, gives me a small smile and waves. I'm about to smile back when she turns around and places her lips on his.

I want to get out of this car and pull her away from him. I shouldn't have offered to pick her up here. I look away, not wanting to see anymore, my teeth clenched. Minutes later, the passenger door opens, and she slides in, smelling of vanilla.

"Hey, thanks for picking me up."

"Yeah."

"Um ... how about we go to the beach? This time of night shouldn't be too crowded, and we can talk."

"You don't want to get something to eat?" I ask. I came here right from work, and I'm starving.

"I packed some sandwiches." It's then I notice the small basket on her lap.

I give her a nod and back out of the driveway.

Flashback Chapter

Ultrasound Day

Dray

The more pregnant Melissa gets, the more she glows. She's cranky as fuck, but it doesn't faze me. I'm used to her moods.

As we grow closer every day, part of me feels guilt, guilt for not telling her about my past, for not being able to let her in on my real job. At the same time, hiding the truth from her, protects her. As for my past, well, that protects both of us. It's not the type of shit I ever want to bring up again, and since it's over and done with, it's not something that ever needs to be out in the open.

I reach over the console and grab her hand, giving it a squeeze. "You doing okay?" I ask her.

"Ugh, no. I have to pee so bad. Why the hell do they make you drink so much water? Especially someone like me, who has an extremely small bladder. Fuuuck, I'm gonna piss my pants." She complains.

I chuckle. "Just go to the bathroom when we get in there." We're on our way for an ultrasound, hoping to find out the sex of our child.

"They told me not to pee before the appointment. They'll let me go after." She whimpers as I drive over a pothole. "I'm so hungry, I need to eat."

"Right after the appointment, we'll get you some food. I promise." I assure her.

"I want a burger from McDonald's, a poutine from Dairy Queen, and I would love a chicken wrap from KFC." I shake my head, at least all three restaurants are close to each other.

Ten minutes later we pull into the Imagining Services parking lot. "I'm not gonna make it, Dray. I need to pee so bad."

"Come on, we'll sign in, and you'll be able to pee soon."

I hold back a laugh as she waddles in front of me. She's not that big, but she's trying to not piss herself while she moves. Once we're signed in, we don't even need to take a seat. She's apparently first appointment of the afternoon, so they bring us right back.

The jelly goes on her stomach, and she doesn't even flinch. "It's not cold?" At all her doctors' checkups that shit apparently is freezing and she flinches.

"We keep our jelly in the warmer." The technician tells us as she puts the doppler on her stomach. "Oh."

"Oh? Oh what? What's going on? Something wrong?" I panic.

She laughs. "No nothing, however, I'm going to have to get you to go to the bathroom, your bladder is way too full for us to see anything."

Melissa glares at her and then to me. "Told you!" she wipes off her stomach and stomps out to find a bathroom.

Twenty minutes later, after the technician finishes doing all her measurements and stuff she asks us if we want to know what we're having.

"It's a girl." Is printed it big letters on the screen. Tears fill my eyes and I look to Melissa.

"We're having a girl."

She smiles brightly. "Yeah."

"God, I love you," I tell her and help wipe up her stomach. Before she gets up, I rest my hands on her belly, and give it a kiss. "Daddy is gonna spoil the hell out of you."

"Can I get up now? I have to pee again." Melissa pouts.

Laughing I help her sit up and we head out.

Chapter 30

Melissa

This is so much harder than I thought it would be. After Caden convinced me to go out and really talk with Dray, I was willing to just move on. Just be with Caden because I was happy. But ever since we talked, I've been thinking about it more and more, and in a way, he's right. I really do need to talk to Dray, to see where my feelings truly do lie.

I almost feel guilty, though, as if I'm cheating on Caden right now. I fell for him so hard and fast, I didn't even give Dray a second thought, but now here I am, alone in a car with him as we drive to the beach, and my stomach has butterflies in it.

I'm so torn.

Should I try to give Dray a second chance, give Mikayla what she deserves, both her parents together? My head is torn.

I hand him the sandwiches as we sit down, across from each other, at the picnic table and he hastily takes them, eating them quickly, only glancing at me when he notices I'm not touching my own.

"You're not hungry?" he asks, frowning.

I shake my head. "No," I sigh, "This is a bit awkward."

"It's only awkward if you make it that way, pretty sure you did that before you even got into my car."

I frown at him. "What do you mean by that?"

"Kissing that asshole in front of me?" He's starting to get angry, and this isn't what I wanted tonight.

"Look, you have to understand that he's a part of my life now, that's not going to change." And it's not, even if I decide to not be with Caden, he's part of my dad's club, we'll always be in each other's lives in some way.

"I wish I could change that." He takes a napkin and wipes his face, tossing it on the table. "I love you, Melissa. Yeah, I fucked up, we both know how badly I fucked up. But I'm here, I want a chance to make this right. Right with you, be there for my kid. I just want a chance to prove myself to you."

I swallow as I feel the tears coming. "Dray, I still love you, too, but this is so much more complicated now."

"What's complicated about this? You just told me you still love me."

"Because I love him too," I confess.

His face gets red and he leans forward. "*Bullshit!* You've only known him a few months, you've known me since you were eighteen. That's gotta count for something."

"It does, Dray. I just don't know what I want right now. When I think about him leaving me, I feel as if my heart is shattering, but when I think about you, I just ... I just miss you so damn much. I'm so torn."

His face falls at my words. "This what you wanted to talk about then? Wanted to let me know you weren't breaking up with him?"

"No, actually um, I was hoping we could date. But not exclusively, well, yes, but no. Shit, this isn't making sense. I want to date you both of you."

He stares at me in shock, trying to absorb my words. He clears his throat after the silence stretches on for too long. "What's he think of this?"

I bite my lip. "It was his idea actually."

His eyes bug out so much I'm scared for a moment they'll fall out. "Are you serious? How can he be okay with this?"

"He just wants what is best for me."

"What's best for you would to just be with me, we both know it."

"So, you're saying no?"

I can hear his teeth grinding as he glares at me. "A smart man would say fuck this and leave, but if this is the only way I can have you, for now, I'll go along with it." He stands up and walks around the table.

As I'm about to ask him what the hell he's doing, he pulls me up from my seat and slams his mouth down on mine. As his tongue finds mine, I groan. "Fuck, I missed this," he mumbles against my lips.

Chapter 31

Slammer

"Slow down, shitface. Thought things were going good with you and my kid."

"I fucked up. Told her to give that bastard a shot, and I saw him kiss her. So I'm drinking myself stupid until I lose the urge to blow his goddamned head off." Anara showed up at the house to take over babysitting duties after I got a call from Rage letting me know the club was having a party after Church. As I drove out here to the clubhouse, I took the long way, and what I saw on that beach, *fuck*, I wanted to kill. I wanted to go right over there and rip them apart.

"You go doing some dumb shit like that then you'll end up dead or back behind bars and Melly won't have you at all. There are other ways to cut the head off a snake."

"You can't want him around either, the fucker is a cop."

"I know, I also know he's currently investigating the Jacks Devils. They catch wind of that, he'll end up dead and it won't have anything to do with you or me."

"So, what you're saying is to just sit back and not worry about fuck all because the Jacks are taking care of an Untamed problem."

"I'm not saying shit, but we all know the last three detectives that were investigating them ended up dead."

He's right, but that shit might not be a good thing for us, though. As much as I want Dray out of the picture, I don't want him dead for Mikayla's sake. She deserves to have a father and doesn't need her stepfather to be the reason he's dead.

Hangman pats my shoulder and gives me a squeeze. "Forget about what you saw tonight, enjoy the party." He walks off, grabbing a blonde away from Dirty and drags her to the back rooms.

"Well hey there, handsome. Haven't seen you around lately, I've missed you." Great, I've avoided parties lately because I didn't want this sort of shit happening. Especially not with Crystal.

"What do you want?" I ask, not looking at her, and continue sipping at my drink.

"Word around the club is you are banging the President's daughter."

"Yep."

"That's a shame, I never thought you would be the one off the market."

I shrug. "Shit changes."

"Doesn't have to." she sidles up closer and shoves her tits against me, tits I've fucked hundreds of times. Of all the women in the club she was the only one I kept going back for more to. Bitch is a wildcat in the sack. Since Melissa, though, I've never even gave Crystal a second thought. "We can still keep doin what we've been doin, she doesn't have to know."

As she tries to get into my lap, I shove her away, noticing she's not wearing panties. Her perfectly waxed pussy on display. I quickly look away and shake my head. "I'm not straying, I'm with Melissa, the woman I'm gonna marry and have kids with, so fuck off."

She huffs and stomps her foot, sliding a hand down to cup herself. "As soon as I found out you were coming tonight, I got all fresh and clean just for you. You really turning me down?" She looks at me in disbelief.

"You were a great fuck, best of all the women in this club, but I've found better, and I ain't ruining shit with her for a quick lay with you."

"Fine, whatever." She stomps off and goes to another member, grabbing his hand and placing it on her cunt. She looks at me and smirks, and when she doesn't get the reaction she was hoping for, she glares at me. I turn away from the scene and finish my drink.

"I'm out," I say to Dirty.

"Me too, I'll follow ya, take Anara home."

I grin at him. "Sure that's all you're gonna do?"

"I gotta start somewhere, man."

Climbing on our bikes we roar out of the compound.

Chapter 32

Melissa

A month later

I know I need to look at this test, but I'm scared of the fact I don't know who my baby's father is. I discovered last week that I was late, at the same time I thought back and realized even last month I only spotted lightly. Then at the same time I realized that I've had unprotected sex with two men. Two men I love, care about, and can't friggin' choose between.

I'm highly positive this baby is Caden's, but it could also very well be Dray's. Fuck, I'm such a whore. What will they both think?

They agreed to let me date them both, but I don't know if they realized I was fucking them both too. The first time I had sex with Dray was the night he picked me up so we could talk. Mostly I let my vagina do the talking. She's such a bitch. I know that news will destroy them both. Every time I was with Caden, I avoided Dray for a few days, every time I was with

Dray, I would avoid Caden. Except for two weeks ago, when I had my date with Dray, we made love, and I came home and let Caden fuck me on his bike.

I'm suck a fucking slut.

How did my life become this? How did everything get so damn complicated?

I finally turn the test over on the counter and look at it. It's positive. I'm having another baby.

**

Slammer

I wake up and notice Melissa's not in bed next to me and see the light on across the hall in the bathroom. Her side of the bed is cold, which means she's been in there a while. Getting up I knock lightly on the door before opening it, and see Melissa holding something in her hand.

Her head snaps up quickly and her eyes widen, and I notice tears in them.

"What's wrong? You okay?" I kneel in front of her, my hands on her knees.

"I'm pregnant," she whispers.

I'm going to be a Dad. *Fuck yeah*. I grin at her and notice she doesn't smile back.

"I don't know if this baby is yours or Dray's," she sobs.

I wrap my arms around her. Fuck, that kills, knowing she's also been sleeping with him. I knew she was, but it was never something she came right out and said. Hearing her say it now, *fuck.* "Everything will be okay."

"How can it be okay? I'm such a slut!" she sobs into my neck.

I shove her away slightly and glare at her. "You're not a slut, don't fuckin' say shit like that again. We'll figure everything out, I promise. You need to talk to Dray, though. As much as I hate to admit it, he has a right to know. There are tests we can do before the baby is born, but I don't give a fuck, I feel it in my gut that this child is mine."

She cries more, hugging me tight. "Why are you so friggin' perfect? Why can't you be a jerk, so I can have at least one thing bad to say about you."

I chuckle.

I stand up, pulling her with me, and carry her into her bedroom. Setting her on the bed.

She might be feeling all sorts of fucked up right now, but I have the need to fuck her, to celebrate the child I'm positive we created together.

A sob hiccups in her chest, and I crash my mouth down on hers hard, cutting it off.

"No more tears tonight, baby. Let me love you," I tell her, pulling her shirt over her head, exposing those tits I love so much.

Laying her back on the bed I take my time kissing my way up her thighs, teasing at her pussy, and moving on up her torso until I find her mouth again.

"This baby…" I kiss her lips as my hands rub over her stomach. "This baby is a blessing. A life we made."

She starts to remind me it might not be mine, but I'm not hearing any of that shit. Dray doesn't get to be between us tonight.

"Shh. I told you. I feel it with every fiber of my being, this baby is mine. Mine." I thump my chest and claim her mouth again.

Sliding my dick inside her, I feel at home. There is nowhere I would rather be but right here with her.

Chapter 33

Dray

Spending time with Melly has been amazing, I've missed her, but I've noticed the last few date nights we've had she's been off. I don't know if it's because she's also dating that fucking biker prick and he's muddling her head before she comes out with me, or if it's something else. I don't want to ask, because I'm scared she's going to tell me she chooses him.

I give her hand a squeeze as we walk out of the movie theater. I decided to take her to that new Strangers movie she's been wanting to see. I didn't really care for it, as I'm not into the horror genre, but she loves it. I wanted to make her happy, only I noticed she barely watched it while we were there. Hell, at one point, she fell asleep and even gagged when I tried to share some popcorn.

"Dray, we need to talk," she says as I climb in the driver's seat.

My heart drops, and I fear this talk is going to kill me.

I swallow deeply. "What about?"

She sighs and turns to look at me. "This wasn't planned, and I'm so sorry for that."

Fuck, she's gonna do it, she fell in love with Slammer and wants him over me.

"I'm pregnant."

Wait, *what?*

I stare at her, trying to take in what she's saying.

"Hello? I said I'm pregnant."

Holy shit. A grin lights up my face. "We're having another baby?" Now Slammer can be out of the picture, and fuck if that doesn't make me happier than I've ever been.

There is no smile on her face though.

"What? What's wrong? This is good news."

She shakes her head and turns away from me. "It's just that ... *well*."

The blood in my veins freeze when I suddenly realize that she's trying to tell me she's pregnant, just not with my kid. I want to punch something, kill something. This can't be happening.

"It's Slammer's," I state, my voice cold.

"I don't know," she whispers.

Well, fuck. I knew she was with him, I just didn't realize that while I was fucking her she was fucking him at the same time. I thought it was just us. I don't know what to say right now, and If I open my mouth to talk to her, I'm gonna hurt her more than I ever have.

I start up the car and drive her home in silence. As I pull into the driveway, she turns to me before opening her door. I refuse to look at her.

"I'm sorry, Dray. I feel like such a slut right now, and not knowing who the father of this child is makes that so much worse." *That's because right now you are a fucking slut*, I want to say. "There are tests we can take if you want to know before the baby is born." Again, I say nothing. I hear her sigh. "I'll talk to you later," she says softly as she gets out.

Fuck her. How could she do this to us? I get her and I not using condoms, but why the fuck isn't she smart enough not to use a condom with a dirty biker?

As I take off down the street, I look in my rear-view mirror and see Slammer pull into the driveway. Fuck, if that doesn't kill a little more. Does he do that all the time? Go to her after she's been with me. Does he fuck her after she fucks me?

Goddamn them! I slam my fist down on the steering wheel hating them both a little. He gets to play house with my goddamned family and all I am getting is his sloppy seconds. I don't know if I am cut out for this. Knowing she sees him all the time and now may be carrying his child stabs me in the gut.

I pull out my phone, letting anger get the best of me and fire off a text.

Do I need to get checked for STDS?

What?! -M

You been fucking that dirty biker and me. You said you're pregnant. When was the last time you were tested? I saw him pulling in after I dropped you off.

I'm sorry. I thought you were okay with things. -M

Maybe I'm not okay with any of it, Melly. This shit is doing my head in.

I don't fuckin' need this shit. I don't wait for her to text back before shutting my phone off. Fuck this.

Flashback Chapter

Mikayla's birth

Melissa

God, this hurts. "Why the fuck won't you give me all the drugs?!" *I scream at the nurse that just walked into the room.*

"I'm sorry, but it seems everyone in the city is giving birth today, and we only have one anesthesiologist on staff this evening."

Cori must know I'm about to go off on this nurse because she gets in my face. "Just breathe damn it. Seriously. You're giving me a headache." *The moment those words are out of her mouth she pales and backs away.*

"Giving you a headache? I'm giving you a headache?"

She puts her hands up. "It got you from going fucking psycho on the nurse!"

She has a point. "Where the fuck is Dray?"

"He's getting a bite to eat with Blake, remember. You've been screaming for the last four hours, and not fully ready to

push yet, so he needed a damn break. Plus, I think during one of your contractions, you sprained his hand."

"Serves him right, stupid bastard did this to me in the first place."

"You ever gonna marry him?"

Dray has asked me repeatedly during the pregnancy to marry him, but I say no each time. I want to marry him, but being a pregnant bride wasn't something I ever wanted. Now that I'm having the baby, the next time he asks me, I'm going to say yes. But even then, I want to wait. I want to be together without being pregnant. I want to knock off all this baby weight I gained. That's not too much to ask for is it? If he loves me and is serious about marrying me, he'll agree.

"Mother fucker!" another stupid contraction pulls me out of my wedding thoughts. "I need those god damned drugs now!"

The nurse I screamed at earlier comes back in and takes a look. "Oh, I'm just going to go get the doctor."

I turn to Cori, who is wiping a cold wet cloth on my face. "What's that mean?"

"I think it's time. I'm gonna get the guys back up here. When it's time to start pushing, do you want it to be just you and Dray?"

"No, I need you here too."

"Then I'll stay. I'll be right back, I'm just going to let everyone know."

Ten minutes later in comes my doctor with Dray and Cori behind him.

Doctor Gregg claps his hands. "It's time."

Dray and Cori stand on each side of me.

"Wait, it can't be time, I need the drugs!"

"No can do. The Anesthesiologist got pulled into a surgery, and this baby is ready."

"Dray, I can't do this." I sob.

"Babe, you can do anything."

"After this you're not gonna love me anymore. My vagina is going to be loose and gross, looking like a nasty ass burger from Arby's."

Cori snorts and I twist my head to glare at her.

"It's legit gonna be like throwing a giant sausage down a double wide hallway. We'll never be able to have sex again. Neither one of us will feel it."

Dray's lips twitch and he shakes his head. "Stop. Everything will be perfect. Now bring my baby into the world."

With Cori and Dray by my side, I do just that.

And now we're both cleaned up, while I hold our beautiful little girl in my arms.

"Daddy, wanna hold her?" I smile up at Dray and hold her out to him.

He wipes a tear from under his eye and takes her from me. God, there is nothing more beautiful than seeing a man hold his child for the first time.

Chapter 34

Melissa

A week later

Having to tell Dray about my pregnancy was hard. His reaction was so much different than Caden's. It has me questioning everything. Part of me wants to take a step away from both men, but the thought of being away from Caden has me physically in pain.

I haven't heard from Dray in a week, he sees Mikayla every other day, but he goes through my dad to do so. It's weird, and I feel somewhat wrong that I haven't really missed him.

Caden, on the other hand, has been here constantly, and we even went to my doctor's appointment together.

Right now, Mikayla and Caden are at the park, it's just me at home. Which is good because I'm about to video chat with my sister, I just really need her advice, maybe she can help me out.

"Hey lil sissy, what's shaking," Cori says, huge smile on her face.

"Everything," I tell her as I hold back my tears.

"Start talking. You know you can talk to me about anything."

So I do. I tell her all about Caden and how amazing he's been. Then I tell her about Dray and what's been going on, finishing off with telling her I'm pregnant and how the men reacted.

"I'm a slut, aren't I?"

Cori glares at me. "How can you be a slut when you were up front and both men knew? That doesn't make you a slut. Don't let me hear that shit come outta your mouth again. Now, as for the men, it's clear to me who you want, Melissa. You and Dray have history, a child, but your relationship has always been a shitty one. Hell, the first time he fucked you, he fucked another chick minutes later, like you meant nothing. Then it turns out he had a wife with two kids; although, they ended up *not* being his kids, but still. Then, of course, his lie about his job. Your whole relationship has been a struggle. But you two powered through and eventually got your shit together. But ask yourself this, can you see a future without Caden? A good man that has never once lied to you, that treats your daughter like his own, a man that puts you first."

My chest aches. "No," I say softly. "It hurts to think about that."

"There you go, you have your answer, because you've never felt that way about Dray. He's a good man. He has his moments anyways, but he's not your forever."

She's right, Dray is my past. We'll always have a relationship because of our daughter, but Caden is my future. It's a future I don't want to let go of.

"Thank you, Cori, now that's out of the way, hold up my nephew! I wanna see him!"

She laughs and leaves the screen to get him. When she comes back, I can't help but stare at him, he looks so much like Cori, it's sort of creepy. "Andrew Jasper. Meet your Auntie Melly."

"Aww, So adorable! And you named him after Angel? What'd he think of that?"

"Don't tell anyone, but he totally teared up. But I wouldn't have named him anything else. Angel and the club saved us, raised us, hell, Trevor is your Uncle, so it's the least I could do."

We talk a little longer and finally hang up when I realize the time. Today I go over a color scheme and design patterns for my restaurant that is finally built. Now just the inside needs to get all done up, and I'll be ready for business.

Once I'm finished with this meeting, I'm going to see Dray and let him know we're over for good. Caden is the man I need and want in my life, and every day he proves how much I mean to him, as well as Mikayla.

Chapter 35

Dray

Marcus slams a file down on my desk. "Got something on those Jacks Devils finally, need you on this as soon as you can. Warrants are all there, pick a team and get out."

Nodding I flip the case file open. Thumbing through the pages, I try to focus, except all I can think about is how Melissa told me last night we were done. Said she couldn't imagine a life without her precious fucking Caden.

That bastard is the only thing standing between me and the family I am supposed to have. Melissa was supposed to be mine, but he got in the way. Spouting his bullshit about how no matter what, this baby she carries will be his. Guy comes off as a goodie fucking two shoes but looking at his record I know he's not. There has to be a way to get him out of Melissa's life and her back into mine.

After the shit I went through with my brother, I won't raise another man's' child, I can't go through that shit again. Honestly, I don't even want to know who the father is. Shit cuts too damn deep. My wounds are still wide open from the kids I had to walk away from. But Melissa is crazy if she thinks I am giving her and my daughter up so easily. No. I want Slammer gone. For good. Maybe even six feet under.

Slamming the files shut, I assemble my team and we leave. Half an hour later, we're pulling through the Jacks Devils compound gates.

Before I fully make it out of my car door, shots are being fired.

Crouching down behind my door, I shout out, "Put your weapons down."

I hear another officer radio back to the station that shots are fired, and we'll have to return fire. I peek to the side and take aim, shooting one of the club members in the leg. Instantly, he drops to the ground in pain, but it doesn't stop him from just firing wildly around the compound.

"They aren't gonna stop shooting at us, what do we do?" Officer Dunlop shouts at me from his spot behind his squad car.

"Has someone called in for backup?" I ask.

"Yeah, they should be here—" He's cut off, and I look back at him, to see blood pooling in his mouth.

"Officer Down! I repeat Officer Down," I say into my radio. Fuck this isn't going the way it was supposed to.

"Backup is en route, hold them off the best you can."

I look around and fire off a shot at anyone wearing a biker cut. I don't see their faces, I pretend they are that bastard, Slammer, who stole my family right out from under me.

I crouch-walk over to Dunlop to see if I can find the bleeding to stop it, and realize he was shot in the back. "Fuck! We're surrounded," I shout to the other officers as gunfire continues to pop off all around me. There is nowhere to dig in for safety. My car is shot up and there is no cover to get behind unless I hide beneath Dunlop's body.

I watch as two more of my men get taken out, and quickly stand up and start firing at anyone I can hit. If I'm going out, I'm gonna take as many of these fuckers as I possibly can with me. I won't go out hiding like a coward. I took an oath and I will uphold it.

Searing pain takes over, as bullets enter my flesh, that's all I can feel right now. I notice the blood pouring to the ground as I drop to my knees. I can taste it in my mouth as it fills up. As the darkness takes over me, my last thoughts are of my daughter. Her sweet smile. Hearing her calling me Daddy. The day she was born. It all flashes through my mind as I drop to the ground. I'm going to miss her sweet smell. All I can think is how I'm going to miss her growing up, her wedding, and how I'll never get to tell her I love her ever again. My eyes flutter as I hear sirens in the distance. A hand reaches down and pulls my head back, as I choke on my own blood.

The bastard smiles smugly at me as a blurry haze clouds my vision.

A Jacks Devil looks me in the eyes and then there is nothing as he slices my throat.

Chapter 36

Slammer

Melissa and I are on the couch, watching a documentary about some serial killer, when her phone rings.

"Hello?" She answers. "Yes, this is she."

Her face pales, and she drops the phone.

"What's wrong?" I ask, pulling her into me.

Tears fall down her face, and I can't keep up with wiping them away.

"It's Dray, he's dead," she says brokenly, choking on her words.

I kiss the top of her head. "I'm so sorry, Melissa. I'm so sorry, baby."

"This is all my fault. This morning, the last thing I told him was that I chose you, and now he's dead. I did this," she sobs into my chest.

My heart feels full, happy, wanting to burst to know she chose me. "Melissa, this isn't your fault. What did they say on the phone?"

"That he was working a case, and the whole team was gone."

I know exactly what happened. Hangman called it. The Jacks Devils took him out. This makes me wonder if Hangman will go after them harder now, or if he'll just let it go. We got what we wanted out of the situation, but for Melissa we'll have to do something or at least say we will.

"They want me to identify the body, I guess I was listed as his next of kin."

"You don't have to do that, I can do it."

"Really?" She sniffles. "Are you sure? I don't think I want to see him like that."

I kiss her head. "Don't worry about it, your dad and I will take care of everything. I promise, the guy in charge of the morgue is actually a member of the club, so it won't be a problem."

She sobs against my chest harder, and it kills me. I wish I could take her pain away.

I wipe at her tears, but they aren't slowing. I know part of her loved him because they had a child together. I can't begrudge her this as I rub soothing circles on her back.

**

"Everything good?" I ask Hangman as I walk into his office a few hours later.

"Yep, it's all been dealt with. Also contacted Melissa's sister and Trevor, they'll all be coming down for the funeral. Trevor said he'll contact the rest of Dray's family so we can start arrangements for the funeral next week."

"What about the Jacks though, we just gonna let them get off with this?"

"Don't worry about the Jacks, it's being handled. You just go handle my kid. She needs you more than I do right now."

**

Melissa

The Funeral

God, I fucking hate this. This whole week leading up to this day has been so damn overwhelming. My sister, her husband, and my nephew showed up four days ago, followed by the entire Angels Warriors club. It's been a godsend to have my entire family here with me.

As I place a flower on Dray's casket, I'm tapped on the shoulder. I turn around and see a beautiful black woman, who smiles sadly at me. "I'm Dray's ex-sister-in-law, Layla, I hope it's okay we came."

"We?"

She tilts her head at the children behind her. "This is Laura and Luca, Dray's niece and nephew." *Oh shit,* these are the children Dray thought were his until he found out the horrible truth. They are stunning, both of them. For a moment I wonder if their mother is here, but I don't see her.

"I'm sorry for your loss," I tell the kids. They come close to me and wrap me up in a hug.

Laura tightens her hold on me. "He loved you so much, I'm sorry for everything that's happened."

"We'll be having a party after he's in the ground at my dad's place, you guys are invited if you'd like to come?"

Layla gives me another smile and looks to the kids. "Our flight leaves later this afternoon, we only wanted to say our goodbyes and pay respects to Dray, just one last time. I have to get back home to my kids. But thank you for the offer."

I nod, give her a sad smile and look to the kids again. I understand Dray leaving his wife, but looking at these children, I don't get how he could have just abandoned them. Hell, if I had known about them myself before the fuckfest that was supposed to be our wedding day, I would have encouraged and demanded Dray to go see them.

"It was good to finally meet you guys. I'm sorry." Luca's eyes fill with tears, and he gives me a chin lift as he walks away. Laura looks back at me after watching her brother leave.

"It was nice to meet you too. I should go check on him."
She points over her shoulder at her brother. She looks to Layla
and nods, and they leave.

**

I stand around the backyard just taking in everything. Half
of the Untamed decided not to come, which is probably a good
thing, considering the Angels Warriors are here. Everyone
seems to be getting along at least.

"Hey sis," Cori says, coming up to me. "How you
feeling?"

"I'm sad, but there's nothing I can do about that except
just move along. Ya know."

She gives my arm a squeeze. "You know I love you,
right? You're my favorite little sister in the universe."

I used to say I was her only sister when she would say
that, but now I can't, since Lilly is her big sister.

"I love you too, and you're my favorite big sister in the
world." Cori looks over the yard and watches Caden play with
her son and Mikayla. "He's good with her, and him, but
especially you."

"Yeah he is."

"I'm glad you met him. I'm happy for you, sis. But I do
have a problem," she sasses, hands on her hips.

I raise a brow. "What'd I do now?"

"I miss you, so we're going to make a pact, twice a year, we need to get together."

"You got a deal, I missed you too." I grab her and pull her in for a hug.

"Alrighty then, enough with the sad shit, had enough of this to last a lifetime. Tell me about your restaurant."

I laugh and loop my arm in hers as we walk towards our family, and I fill her in.

Later on, as I am sitting with Caden, I look up at the sky and hope that wherever Dray is, he knows that Caden and I will do our best to give Mikayla a good life. The best life. I won't let her forget that he's her dad and that he died doing what he loved.

Caden's lips brush along my shoulder. "I love you, Melissa. I promise you, I'm going to make you so damned happy. I'm going to make you my wife."

Twisting around I stare at him in shock. "Are you asking me to—"

He presses a finger to my lips. "No, baby, I'm telling you." He grins and then he slams his mouth down on mine.

Epilogue

Many Years later

Melissa

Why am I doing this again? Damn Caden and his sperm. I swear the fucker wants to keep me knocked up forever. After having our son Jason Vincent, which we found out at his birth was indeed Caden's child, I was pregnant exactly six weeks later. As soon as we got the all clear from the doctor he pounced on me, and bam, knocked up. And two months after our daughter Rachelle Hilary was born, again, knocked up, and now here I am, two weeks over due, finally having this baby.

"Caden, I hate you for this."

He grins at me and winks. That ass.

Since we got married a month after Dray's funeral, everything has completely changed. Caden adopted Mikayla and gave her his last name, but we always make sure to remind her of who her father was. Dray might not have been who I was to end up with, but his death hurt. He shouldn't have died the way he did. The club took their revenge, by getting the man who put the killing bullet in Dray, but their war with the Jacks Devils is far from over as far as I know, considering they are rival clubs.

Caden no longer goes by Slammer, and he's not even part of the club anymore, at least not in the way he once was.

He told me I changed his life and he didn't want to be doing shit that could send him away from me for any reason. My dad, surprisingly, was okay with it. He told me that he'd do anything for me, and if that meant letting Slammer out, then so be it.

My restaurant is doing amazing. With help from the club, we got things up and running before Jason was born. Caden and my dad took care of the hiring process, so I wouldn't have to worry about a thing. The shitty part about it is that I've barely worked there myself. With popping out kids and being pregnant, I've barely spent any time at work. And I hate that.

That's why after this baby, I've told Caden that if he wants more children we need to wait a few years, because I so badly want to do what I was meant to do with my restaurant. I want to create dishes, bake, get to know my staff and interact with my patrons. He reluctantly agreed, but not without a shit load of pouting.

I love him so much. I swear this huge scary man is the biggest softy in the world.

"This next one, you have to bare down push hard, don't stop until I say," the doctor says from between my legs.

After four more pushes, a screaming baby is finally out of me. "It's a girl!"

"Fuck," Caden mutters under his breath, causing me to glare at him. "What? Jason and I are completely outnumbered here. This sucks."

"It's your own damn fault, your sperm likes making girls." Shaking my head at him, I say, "Maybe the next one will be a boy?"

He smiles so big I swear his face will split. "Sounds like a plan."

"But not for a few years this time!" I demand of him.

"Whatever," he grumbles as he watches our new daughter get cleaned up.

After we cuddle and pass around daughter I look at Caden. "What should we name her?"

Without looking at me, he leans in close and kisses her forehead. "Sadie Draya." My heart stutters at the name and tears swim in my eyes.

"It's perfect," I whisper.

He stands up and goes to the door. "I'll go bring in your dad, the kids, and your sister."

I smile, thanking him.

Cori and I, I hate to say this, aren't as close as we once were. And honestly, it's only because of the distance. Instead of spending every day practically together, it's only twice a year now, a week each time. The distance sucks, but we're both finally grown enough to not need each other as we once did. I miss her all the time, of course, but I'm so happy in where I'm at right now, I wouldn't change it for anything.

And seeing my sister overcome all she did, and become who she is now, I don't think she would either.

When we get together, she even treats Hangman as her own father, and it's probably because she knows what he did for us when it came to our mother. She's grateful for it, even though she thought Mom's death was overkill on his part.

Caden

The kids all gather around Melissa and smile at their new baby sister. Fuck my heart feels full.

"Thank you for loving her," Cori says, coming up behind me.

"Trust me, loving her is the easiest thing in the world."

And it is. I wouldn't change our twisted-up love story for anything.

The End

Bonus Epilogue

Hangman

"Hangman," I bark into my phone.

"Paperwork has been looked over and signed, you got what you wanted, I got what I wanted. We're done."

Chaos, the president of the Jacks Devils, and I made a deal. He got rid of my problem and I would give him my bar in Nova Scotia. His club is dominant there, and he's wanted us out for years. With the deal we made, we both got what we wanted.

I hang up the phone, toss it to my desk, and lean back in my chair. I did what I had to do, and I would do it all over again if I need to. There was no way in fuck I was gonna let Dray have my daughter. Making the deal with the Devils, wasn't something I ever wanted to do. But this was one that I couldn't not do. Not without Melissa knowing it was me. It was easier to have her think another club took him out. A club he was investigating, instead of knowing her own father was the one that did it.

Not even Slammer knows what I did. Fuck, the only other person that knows is Rage, and that's how it's gonna stay.

No matter what my kids might say, I'm not a good man. Never was. And I wouldn't change who I am for anyone. I got rid of a problem, a problem that would have caused a shit storm in my family and my club. I stare at the photo on my desk, of a pregnant Melissa and Slammer smiling down at her, me holding up Mikayla beside them, on their wedding day. Yeah, I made the right fuckin' call.

Coming up next – No dates and in no real order, it's just whatever finishes first

Hangman – The Untamed Angels book 1 – Hangman's Story

You Break Me – The Prospect Series book 2 with Glenna Maynard

Yet to be Titled – A Being Yours Novella book 4

Grab Book 1 of the Treyton Sisters Duet – Twisted Up In You – on Amazon

Surviving a harsh upbringing, Corinne Treyton's new life comes courtesy of the Angels Warriors MC. No one will ever use her body again, unless she wants them to. Cori, a party girl, doesn't believe in relationships, but she'd be willing to try if only Blake, who happens to be her boss, could really see her for who she is. She hides her lifestyle from him, afraid he would think less of her.

Blake Lexington has crushed on Cori since the day she started working for him. He knows a bit about her past, living with the Angels Warriors, and he doesn't care. He refuses to make a move, thinking it will scare off his shy assistant. For years, he's thought she would never be attracted to someone like him.

Finally realizing that he needs to take action, her reaction surprises him. Cori believes he sees her as a slut and wants to use her. Secrets from the past will be revealed, causing everything to unravel.

Will real love bring them together, or is Cori too damaged to give true love a chance?

About the Author

Dawn Martens is a young, spunky Canadian Author. Being a wife to Colin, and a mother to three beautiful little girls (Sarah (2007), Grace (2010), and Ava (2014), hasn't stopped this Canadian Firecracker from pursuing her dreams of becoming a writer! Dawn's number one passion in life is the written word, and she's extremely thankful that she has the ability to share the ramblings from the characters inside of her head with the rest of the world! She also may or may not have the hugest girl crush on Author Kristen Ashley, who is her personal idol and helped inspire Dawn in the beginning of her Indie career.

Connect with Dawn on:

Facebook: https://www.facebook.com/AuthorDawnMartens/

Twitter: @Dawn_Martens

Email: authordawnmartens@yahoo.ca

More from this author

Stand Alones

It's Just Love Not a Time Bomb

The Treyton Sister Duet

Twisted Up In You

Twisted Up In Us

Being Yours Novella Series

Never Letting You Go

Wasn't Supposed To Love You

Don't Want To Lose You

Resisting Love Series

Derek (Book Four)

Angel Warriors MC Trilogy

UnKiss Me

UnTouch Me

UnBreak This Heart

UnLove Me (The Angel Warriors MC Complete Trilogy Box Set)

New Love (Angel Warriors MC Novelette)

Angels Warriors MC Spinoff Serious
Always Was Mine

Co- written with Glenna Maynard
Stand Alone
The Boom

The Prospect Series
You Wreck Me

Co-written with Emily Minton
Renegade Sons MC Series
Renegade Lady
Renegade Reject
Renegade Wedding

Love Song Series
Whiskey Lullaby
Broken
I Hope You Dance
Love Song Series Box Set

Co-written with Chantal Fernando
Resisting Love Series
Chase (Book One)